Don't miss out on any of our books in March.

This month, Lynne Graham brings you
The Italian Billionaire's Pregnant Bride,
the last story in her brilliant trilogy THE RICH, THE
RUTHLESS AND THE REALLY HANDSOME, where
tycoon Sergio Torrente demands that pregnant Kathy
marry him. In *The Spaniard's Pregnancy Proposal*
by Kim Lawrence, Antonio Rochas is sexy,
smoldering and won't let relationship-shy Fleur
go easily! In Trish Morey's *The Sheikh's Convenient
Virgin,* a devastatingly handsome desert prince
is in need of a convenient wife who must be pure.
Anne Mather brings you a brooding Italian who
believes Juliet is a gold-digger in *Bedded for the
Italian's Pleasure.* In *Taken by Her Greek Boss*
by Cathy Williams, Nick Papaeliou can't understand
why he's attracted to frumpy Rose—but her
shapeless garments hide a very alluring woman.
Lindsay Armstrong's *From Waif to His Wife* tells the
story of a rich businessman who avoids marriage—
but one woman's sensual spell clouds his perfect
judgment! In *The Millionaire's Convenient Bride*
by Catherine George, a dashing millionaire needs
a temporary housekeeper—but soon the business
arrangement includes a wedding! Finally, in
One-Night Love Child by Anne McAllister, Flynn
doesn't know he's the father of Sara's son—but
when he discovers the truth he *will* possess her....
Happy reading from Harlequin Presents!

Dinner ^{at}8

Don't be late!

He's suave and sophisticated.

He's undeniably charming.

And, above all, he treats her like a lady....

But beneath the tux, there's a primal, passionate lover who's determined to make her his!

Wined, dined and swept away by a British billionaire!

Catherine George
THE MILLIONAIRE'S
CONVENIENT BRIDE

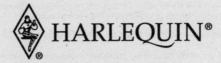

TORONTO • NEW YORK • LONDON
AMSTERDAM • PARIS • SYDNEY • HAMBURG
STOCKHOLM • ATHENS • TOKYO • MILAN • MADRID
PRAGUE • WARSAW • BUDAPEST • AUCKLAND

ISBN-13: 978-0-373-12713-9
ISBN-10:   0-373-12713-8

THE MILLIONAIRE'S CONVENIENT BRIDE

First North American Publication 2008.

This edition published by arrangement with Harlequin Books S.A.

® and TM are trademarks of the publisher. Trademarks indicated with ® are registered in the United States Patent and Trademark Office, the Canadian Trade Marks Office and in other countries.

www.eHarlequin.com

Printed in U.S.A.

All about the author...
Catherine George

CATHERINE GEORGE was born on the border between Wales and England, in a village blessed with both a public and a lending library. Fervently encouraged by a like-minded mother, she developed an addiction to reading early in life.

At eighteen Catherine met the husband who eventually took her off to Brazil, where he worked as chief engineer of a large gold-mining operation in Minas Gerais, which provided a popular background for several of Catherine's early novels.

After nine happy years, the education of their small son took them back to Britain, and soon afterward a daughter was born. But Catherine always found time to read, if only in the bath! When her husband's job took him abroad again she enrolled in a creative writing course, and then read countless novels by Mills & Boon authors before trying a hand at one herself. Her first effort was not only accepted, but voted best of its genre for that year.

Catherine has written well over sixty novels since and has won another award along the way. But now she has come full circle. After living in Brazil and in England's the Wirral, Warwick and the Forest of Dean, Catherine now resides in the beautiful Welsh Marches—with access to a county library, several bookshops and a busy market hall with a treasure trove of secondhand paperbacks!

To Howard, with my love.

CHAPTER ONE

HESTER'S excitement escalated as she neared her goal. She checked the address again, then mounted the steps of one of the tall houses which lined three sides of leafy Albany Square. She rang the bell, gave her name over an intercom and, after a pause, the door was opened by a man who was obviously an employee of some kind, but nothing like her idea of a butler.

He smiled at her pleasantly. 'Good morning, Miss Ward. Come this way.'

Hester followed him along a high-ceilinged hall and up a flight of Bath stone stairs to a large, book-lined study. He held out the chair in front of the desk, told her his employer would be with her shortly and left her alone. Her anticipation at fever pitch, Hester sat, tense, on the edge of the chair. Her preliminary interview had been over coffee in a hotel lounge with John Austin, personal assistant of the owner of this house, but now she was about to meet the man himself.

On the desk a solitary framed photograph faced the window. She hesitated a moment, then turned it towards her and felt a rush of pure adrenaline. Her hunch had been right! The man she'd come to see really *was* her mysterious Mr Jones. And one look at that striking face, with its knife-edge cheekbones and intense dark eyes, sent her straight back to her first encounter with the man smiling down at a child in the photograph.

She had been packing that cold January night when her mother rushed in, radiating urgency.

'Give me a hand, darling. We've got guests.'

Hester stared at her in disbelief. '*What?* At this time of night?'

'I just couldn't say no. It's snowing, and they look exhausted.'

'Honestly, Mother! We're supposed to be closed for the entire month. You should have put the No Vacancies sign out.'

Moira Ward gave her a stern look. 'I want help, please, not a lecture.'

'Right away!' Hester hurried after her mother, down the back stairs to the kitchen. 'Where are they?'

Moira began taking food from the refrigerator. 'Settling into their rooms while I whip up a snack. Mr Jones accepted my offer of sandwiches with such enthusiasm I think it's a long time since either of them had a meal.'

Hester shook her head in disapproval as she buttered bread. 'You're too soft-hearted by half.'

'But not soft-headed,' returned Moira tartly. 'I don't turn away paying guests who offer cash in advance.' She sighed. 'Besides, the poor girl looked ready to drop. I couldn't turn them away.'

'Of course you couldn't!' Hester blew her a kiss. 'What shall I put in these?'

'Slice some of the roast ham from supper, and I'll heat up the rest of my vegetable soup. The girl looked frozen.'

'You want me to take the tray up?'

'Yes, please, darling. I'd rather they knew I'm not alone in the house.'

Hester laughed. 'I doubt that my presence will make much difference if Mr Jones has anything sinister in mind.' Her eyes narrowed. 'Wait a minute. Did you say rooms plural?'

Moira nodded. 'The connecting rooms at the front.'

'So we not only feed these people supper as well as breakfast, we clean the two largest rooms in the house after they've gone!'

'For which I've been paid a handsome sum in advance,' her mother reminded her, and, with a triumphant smile, played her trump card. 'You can have half of it to take back to college.'

Hester laughed as she gave her mother a hug. 'Brilliant! Thanks, Ma. Why aren't they sleeping together, do you think?'

'Ours is not to reason why.' Moira added a tureen of steaming soup to the tray and sent her daughter on her way.

Hester bore her burden with care up the wide staircase, eager to take a look at the couple who'd appealed to her mother's hospitable heart.

The man who opened the first of the garden view rooms smiled as he took the tray and one look at the handsome, haggard face took Hester's breath away.

'Thank you.' His voice was deep, with a timbre that sent shivers down her spine. 'Would you tell Mrs Ward we're deeply grateful?'

'I will,' she said with effort, and pulled herself together. 'You'll find biscuits, coffee, tea and kettle on the desk, and I've brought fresh milk. Can I get you anything else?'

He shook his head as he inspected the tray's contents. 'This is wonderful—and much appreciated.'

'No trouble at all,' she assured him fervently. 'What time would you like breakfast?'

He glanced at the closed connecting door. 'We need to be on our way first thing. Would toast and coffee be possible about seven-thirty?'

'Of course. I'll bring it up.' And bring it willingly if it meant another encounter with the knee-trembling Mr Jones. Plus no dining room to clean afterwards.

Hester went back downstairs in a pink haze. That, she thought reverently, was one mouth-watering male specimen if you liked your men tall, dark and masterful. Which she did. Or would if she knew any. She sighed enviously. The lady with him was very lucky. Her man had charisma in spades.

Moira was drinking tea at the table when Hester went back to the kitchen. 'Everything all right?'

'With the *über*-gorgeous Mr Jones, yes. The connecting door was half closed so I didn't see his lady.'

'If you had, you'd have seen for yourself why I couldn't turn them away. She looks like a ghost, poor thing.'

Hester poured milk into a mug, stirred in squares of chocolate and put it in the microwave to heat. 'He wants breakfast at seven thirty, so I said I'd take it up. But what on earth were they doing out here in January at this time of night? We don't normally do much with passing trade.'

This was true. Most of their customers came via tourist agencies and the Internet.

'Mr Jones said he'd meant to drive overnight,' said her mother, 'but his companion began feeling ill about the time it started to snow. At which point he spotted our sign on the main road and turned up here on the off chance that we had room.'

Hester fluttered her eyelashes. 'I thought Smith was the alias of choice for secret getaways. Do you think Jones is his real name?'

'That's how he signed the register.'

'Pretty anonymous. He could have murdered the woman's husband to run off with her for all we know.'

Moira shook her head. 'I somehow doubt that! But they'll both be gone in the morning, so we'll never know.'

Never say never, thought Hester, her excitement back in full force as she heard footsteps on the stairs. The clock struck the hour in a nearby church steeple to mark the occasion as she rose to face the man who'd made such an impression on her ten years ago that she'd never forgotten him.

Tall and impressive in a formal suit, he looked older and more remote, but the thick black Celtic hair and ink dark eyes were unmistakable—and had exactly the same effect as the first time they'd met. He came towards her, hand outstretched, a slight smile softening the hard, imperious features. 'Connah Carey Jones. I apologise for keeping you waiting.'

Hester took the hand and felt a jolt of heat rush through her like an electric shock. Heart thumping in startled response to the contact, she returned the smile with determined composure. 'Not at all, I was early.'

He waved her back to her chair, then seated himself behind the desk, looking at her in narrow-eyed silence for a long moment before turning to her application.

She tensed. Could he have remembered her? But if he did he made no mention of it as he read through her CV.

'You look young to have so much experience in childcare,' he said at last.

'But, as you see, I'm twenty-seven.' She hesitated. 'Mr Carey Jones, to avoid any possible waste of your time, could you confirm that the post is purely temporary?'

'Certainly. It's for the summer vacation only.' The dark eyes looked up to connect with hers. 'However, there is a complication. Lowri went away to school when she was eight, and would hotly resent the idea of having a nanny again. To get round this, I've told her I'm hiring a temporary house-keeper. Sam Cooper, the man who let you in, actually runs our all male household, but during the school holiday I need a woman on hand to provide Lowri's meals, see to her personal laundry and take her out during the day. Her evenings would be spent with me.'

'I see.' Not that Hester did, entirely. Once she'd discovered the name of her prospective employer, and began wondering if he was the same Mr Jones, she'd put out some feelers through a journalist contact on the *Financial Times* to find out if her hunch was right. But Angus had drawn a blank on personal details. Known as the Welsh Wizard due to his phenomenal success in the world of finance, Connah Carey Jones kept his private life so strictly private there'd been no mention of a wife and child.

He returned to her application. 'Would a Norland-trained nanny with such glowing references object to posing as a house-keeper, Miss Ward?'

'Not in the slightest,' she assured him. 'I have experience in that field too, Mr Carey Jones. After my father died, my mother turned the family home into a successful bed and breakfast operation. I was involved at every level right from the start. I enjoy cooking and did a certain amount of it in my previous post, as I explained to Mr Austin.'

'It would certainly help in this instance,' he agreed, 'but my priority is finding someone trustworthy and competent, who is also young enough to be company for my daughter. It would be necessary to live in for the period of employment, also to furnish the requisite references and agree to a security check.'

'Of course.'

He mentioned the very generous salary offer and looked at her in enquiry. 'Now that you're clear about my requirements, Miss Ward, would you accept the post if it were offered?'

Like a shot.

'Yes, Mr Carey Jones, I would,' she said firmly.

'Thank you for being so straightforward. I'll be in touch as soon as possible.' And, instead of ringing for his butler, he surprised her by accompanying her downstairs to see her out.

Buzzing from her encounter with Mr Jones, Hester set off at a brisk pace to walk back to the house on the hilly outskirts of town. She waved, smiling, when her stepfather threw open the front door before she was halfway up the steep path to the house. 'Hi, Robert.'

He hurried her inside, his kind face expectant. 'How did it go?'

'Quite well, I think, but I'll have to wait to see if I beat the opposition.'

'Of course you will! Moira's popped out for something

missing from the lunch menu, but we'll eat in the garden as soon as she gets back.'

Hester kissed his cheek affectionately, then went out to climb the fire escape stairs to the garage flat Robert Marshall had redecorated to her taste. Hester's chosen career required her to live in with whatever family she worked for, and now the family home had been sold she was deeply grateful to Robert for providing her with the security of a private, self-contained apartment as a base. She gazed out over his steep, beautifully tended garden as she changed into shorts and a halter-neck top, wondering if a second interview was likely. Having met Connor Carey Jones again, she fervently hoped so.

When Moira came back with her shopping, her jaw dropped when Hester, not without drama, announced that her interview had been with the man who'd made such an impression on them both all those years ago.

'I had an idea it might be him, Ma,' she said, smiling triumphantly, 'but I didn't say anything because it sounded so far-fetched. But I was right. The man in need of a temporary nanny for his daughter really is our mysterious Mr Jones.'

'*Amazing!* How did you react when you saw him?'

'Luckily there was a photograph of him with a little girl on his desk, to give me advance warning.'

Moira shook her head in wonder. 'Did he recognise you?'

'Of course not. I've changed a lot since then. Besides, you saw far more of him than I did. They didn't end up leaving early in the morning as they'd planned and I had to get back to college before they left—so I never did meet his lady.'

'He was worried in case she had something infectious. She didn't, as it happened, but she was far too ill to travel, so I let them stay on for a few days until she was better.' Moira smiled reminiscently. 'Mr Jones was very appreciative. He sent me the most wonderful flowers afterwards.'

'Now you've solved your mystery, would you like the job, Hester?' asked Robert.

She nodded fervently. 'I certainly would. But apparently the daughter would object to having a nanny again, so if I did get it I'd have to pose as the temporary housekeeper.'

'No problem for you, darling,' said Moira promptly. 'You've had far more experience of housekeeping than most girls your age.'

'I think the age bit might be the problem. I got the impression he wanted someone a bit older.'

Hester found out sooner than expected. During the evening John Austin rang, asking if it was convenient for her to call back at the house in Albany Square to meet his employer at noon the next day. She raced into the garden to break the news.

'First hurdle over, folks. I've got a second interview tomorrow.'

Hester felt nervous as she mounted the steps to the elegant house in Albany Square the following morning. Which was silly. It wouldn't be the end of the world if she didn't get the job. But, having met Mr Jones again, she was very keen to work for the man she'd had such a crush on when she was a teenager. And the bonus of six weeks generous salary while she was filling in time wouldn't hurt, either. The original plan for the gap between jobs had been a holiday in the South of France, but she'd kept that secret in case it fell through at the last minute. Which it had.

The butler gave her a friendly smile as he opened the door. 'Good morning, Miss Ward. I'll show you straight upstairs.'

This time Connah Carey Jones was waiting at the open study door to greet her.

'Thank you for coming again at short notice.' He led her to the chair in front of the desk. 'To get straight to the point, your credentials tick all the boxes, Miss Ward. I notice you even live here in town.'

'Yes. Though it's actually my stepfather's house.'

His eyes sharpened. 'You don't feel welcome there?'

She shook her head. 'On the contrary, Robert couldn't be kinder.'

When his phone rang he glanced at it, then, with a word of apology, left the room. Hester's tension mounted as she waited for him to come back. It looked as though the job was hers. But first she had to tell him that they'd met before. He obviously didn't remember her. No surprise there. He'd been so worried about his lady at the time he'd had no attention to spare for a chubby teenager with heavy eye make-up and yards of blonde corkscrew curls. She was ten years older now, twenty pounds lighter, and her smooth coiled hair and discreet cosmetics were more in keeping with her job.

Connah Carey Jones came back into the room shortly afterwards and sat behind the desk. 'John has checked your references, Miss Ward, and has also run a security check on your background—'

'Before you go on,' she said, bracing herself, 'I must tell you that we've already met.'

He sat back in his chair, nodding slowly as he trained his eyes on her face. 'I thought you looked familiar, but I couldn't pinpoint why.'

'Until I saw you yesterday,' she said quickly, 'I didn't know we'd met before. I'd read about you in the press, but I'd never seen a photograph—'

'Because I make very sure I keep out of the limelight,' he assured her. 'I'm not a social animal, so where exactly did we meet, Miss Ward?'

'You came knocking on the door of our B & B one night, looking for accommodation.'

He stared at her, arrested. 'That was *your* home?'

'Yes. We were supposed to be closed, but it was snowing, so my mother hadn't the heart to turn you away.'

'And I thanked God for it. I've never forgotten her kindness.' He frowned. 'But I'm afraid I don't remember you.'

'I was the one who brought your trays up.'

'The teenager with yards of hair?' He smiled, surprised. 'You look very different now.'

'Ten years is a long time,' she said wryly.

'It is indeed.' He looked at her in silence for a moment. 'Right. Let's get down to brass tacks, Miss Ward. You and your mother were so kind I'm only too glad to return the favour in some small way. If you want this job, it's yours.'

She smiled warmly. 'Thank you. I promise to take good care of your daughter.'

'Good. Talking of Lowri, you need some details about her.' He looked at his watch. 'Let me give you some lunch while I put you in the picture.'

The meal was served under a vine-covered pergola overlooking a suntrap patio garden at the back of the house.

'May I give you some wine?' asked Connah.

'Thank you. I'm walking today; my car's in for service.'

'You won't need your own car while you're here,' he informed her as he filled glasses. 'Sam Cooper will drive you wherever you need to go. His official job description is butler, but he's a great deal more than that. While Lowri is here with me, his priority is security.'

Hester eyed him, startled. 'You're afraid of kidnap?'

'Afraid isn't the exact term. Let's say I keep a constant guard against the possibility.'

'Does Lowri know this?'

'No.' The handsome face set in grim lines. 'Nor, if humanly possible, do I intend her to find out.'

'But how do you manage when she's at school?'

'I chose one with security as one of its top priorities.'

'But she had a nanny up to that point?'

He nodded. 'Her mother died when she was born, and my

mother brought her up with the help of a girl from the village. When Lowri went away to school Alice stayed on to help my mother for a while, but she got married recently; hence the problem for the school holiday. My mother's recovering from heart surgery and can't take care of Lowri this time.'

Hester looked thoughtful as she helped herself to salad. 'Does Lowri like boarding school?'

'She took to it like a duck to water, thank God. Now,' he added briskly, 'down to business.'

Connah Carey Jones made his requirements very plain. Without letting his daughter feel she was being watched every minute of the day, Lowri's safety was to be Hester's main concern.

'Sam will drive you to the park, or into town for shopping. This last, by the way, is urgent. Lowri needs new clothes. She's growing rapidly, particularly her feet. But you can leave school shoes until the end of the holiday,' he added, with an unexpected touch of economy.

'I shall do my best for her,' she assured him.

He nodded briskly. 'I feel sure you will, Miss Ward. In this household, by the way, we're all on first name terms. Are you happy with that?'

'Of course.'

'Good.' He smiled briefly. 'I hope you enjoy your stay with us. Feel free to ask me for anything you need.' He looked up as Sam appeared with a coffee tray. 'Hester has agreed to work with us during Lowri's school holiday, Sam. I've put your many and varied services at her disposal.'

'Right you are.' Sam gave Hester a friendly smile and set the tray down in front of her. 'I live in the basement flat, so I'm always on hand.'

'Thank you.' Hester smiled at him warmly. 'I'll depend on you to show me the ropes.'

'You can run Hester home later, Sam,' said Connah. 'I'll give you a call when she's ready.' He leaned back, relaxed, as Hester dealt with the coffee. 'This is pleasant. I should eat out here more often.'

'Does Lowri share your evening meal, or should I make supper earlier for her?'

'When I'm home we eat together, to make the most of each other's company. But I'll let you know in good time if I can't make it.'

'Thank you.' She smiled. 'It would also help if you could give me an idea of Lowri's tastes. At her age I was a bit picky.'

He shrugged. 'Lowri will coax for fast food because the school doesn't allow it. Indulge her now and again as a treat, but otherwise just make sure she keeps to a balanced diet. Sam normally shops online, but Lowri might enjoy looking round a supermarket. Choose what you want, pay in cash, and Sam will carry the bags. And right now he'll give you a tour of the house before you leave.' Connah downed his coffee and got up. 'I collect Lowri on Friday, Hester. Are you free to start on Monday morning?'

'Yes. What time shall I come?'

'About eight-thirty. Unfortunately I need to be in London afterwards for a day or two so I'm throwing you in at the deep end. But Sam has my contact numbers.'

'Mr Carey Jones—'

'Connah,' he reminded her.

'I just wanted to ask after your mother.'

'She had a triple heart bypass and her convalescence is worryingly slow. When I fetch Lowri we'll spend time with her before coming back here.' He glanced at his watch and collected his jacket. 'I must be off.'

'Thank you for lunch,' said Hester, as they went back into the house.

'My pleasure.' He beckoned as Sam appeared. 'Show Hester round, then drive her wherever she wants to go. I'll see you on

Monday, Hester. All right, John,' he said, resigned, as his assistant opened the study door. 'Put your whip away, I'm coming.'

'If you're ready, Hester, we'll start at the bottom with my quarters and work up,' Sam suggested.

She followed him down a short flight of stairs to a compact, orderly basement flat. His sitting room doubled as an office, with electronic equipment to screen visitors, and the control panels of a very complicated alarm system.

'Connah's very hot on security,' he explained.

'So I gather. Have you worked for him long?'

'Since I left the military. The lower stairs lead to a cellar Connah converted into a double garage,' Sam added as he led her up to the ground floor into a kitchen with tall sash windows and a door that opened on to the back patio. 'My quarters used to be the kitchen and scullery, and this was the original dining room,' he explained. 'The old butler's pantry leads off it—very handy for the freezer and washing machine and so on.'

'Very nice indeed,' she commented. The large kitchen was fitted with every modern appliance possible, including a state-of-the-art electric range. 'You'll have to give me a teach-in on that before I start producing meals.'

Sam chuckled. 'If I get a share in the result sometimes, no problem. I'm a dab hand with a potato peeler.'

'I'll remember that!' They went up to the next floor and passed by the closed study door to enter a drawing room furnished with the emphasis on comfort and lit by the multi-paned windows typical of Regency architecture. The adjoining dining room was more formal and painted an authentic shade of pale green Hester found cold. The master bedroom on the next floor was part of a suite with a bathroom, dressing room and guest room, Sam informed Hester as they passed by on the way to the top floor.

'You're up here, next to Lowri,' he said, leading the way to two adjoining bedrooms, each with a small bathroom and a view over the trees in the square to the hills encircling the town. 'You wouldn't think so now, but these were the attics at one time. Suit you all right?' added Sam.

Hester nodded, impressed. 'But how is it so cool up here on a hot day like this?'

'Air-conditioning.'

Sam's phone rang as they went downstairs. 'Right you are, Connah. Coming down now. He wants to see you again before you go, Hester,' he added.

Connah looked up as she put her head round the study door. 'Come in and sit down. Is your room satisfactory?'

'Very much so.'

'Good.' He consulted a list. 'Next on the agenda, time off. You're free to go out some evenings when I'm home, Sundays are your own, also the occasional Saturday from noon onwards. You'll have to ring the doorbell to gain entry, but Sam will either be with you or waiting for you, so it's not a problem.' He paused, as though gauging her reaction. 'Or is it?'

'Of course not,' said Hester, though it was, a little. 'Otherwise I'd need the code for your impressive security system.'

'Other than myself, only Sam knows that.'

'Not even Mr Austin?'

'No. John's London based so he isn't here very much, but when he is he rings the bell.' He paused, giving her a very direct look. 'One last point. In your application you say you're single but precisely how single are you?'

Hester felt her hackles rise as she met the intent dark eyes. 'For the time being, totally. There's no danger of gentleman callers, Mr Carey Jones.'

CHAPTER TWO

'I'VE been pronounced fit to take care of Connah Carey Jones's ewe lamb, but not to drive her anywhere myself, nor to be trusted with a key to the house,' Hester announced when she got home. 'Security is a religion with the man. If that's what it means to have loads of money, I'll pass.'

'You can't blame him for wanting to keep his child safe,' said her mother, and shook her head in wonder. 'I'm still amazed that he's the man who turned up on our doorstep in the snow all those years ago. You were very taken with him at the time!'

'You must have been too, to volunteer full board for a few days,' Hester retorted.

'I liked him, yes,' said Moira, and smiled wickedly. 'But I wasn't moonstruck like you, darling.'

'I've been reading up on him,' said Robert, the peacemaker. 'He's one of the new hedge fund breed. He made a packet with an asset management firm he set up with a partner, but eventually sold off his share in the firm to "pursue other interests", but these weren't specified.'

Hester nodded. 'I heard that much from Angus Duff, my journalist chum. Of course I didn't know if the CC Jones he researched was our man, but I somehow had this gut feeling that he might be.'

Moira eyed her narrowly. 'Was that why you were so keen to apply?'

'Of course not. I replied to a box number. It was only when John Austin told me the name of his employer that I had this wild idea that Mr CC Jones might just possibly be our mystery man. But even then my only reason for applying was to earn some extra money before I go to the Rutherfords in October.' Hester smiled in satisfaction. 'While I'm living in Albany Square I'll spend very little, which will do wonders for my rainy day fund.'

'How about time off?' asked Robert.

'Every Sunday, the occasional Saturday, and some evenings when the big white chief is at home.'

'You sound as though you're not so enamoured with him this time round,' said her mother.

'His looks still pack the same punch for me, I admit, but I was rather put off when I found he wasn't willing to trust me with a key to the house,' said Hester tartly. 'He also got a bit personal about my social life.'

'Understandable, with someone as attractive as you,' said Robert.

She smiled at him affectionately. 'But I assured him there would be no gentleman callers—'

'Surely you didn't say that!' exclaimed Moira, rolling her eyes. 'You're not an Edwardian parlourmaid, girl!'

'For a moment he made me feel like one,' admitted Hester, eyes kindling.

'What's he like?' asked Robert curiously.

'Tall, dark and formidable, with hard black eyes that pin you down.'

'Are you *sure* you want to work for him?' demanded Moira.

'Don't worry, Mother, I'm sure I can play Jane Eyre to his Rochester for six weeks, whether I like him or not,' Hester assured her, then grinned. 'And I know he doesn't have a mad wife in the attic because that's where I sleep.'

* * *

Robert drove Hester to the house in Albany Square just before eight thirty on her first day and not only insisted on carrying her luggage up the steps to the front door, but on waiting with her until Sam Cooper appeared.

'Good morning, Sam,' said Hester, smiling. 'This is my stepfather, Robert Marshall.'

Sam held out a hand to Robert. 'Sam Cooper, sir.'

Robert gave him a straight look as he took it, then smiled, obviously satisfied with what he saw. 'Glad to meet you. I'm sure I leave Hester in good hands.' He kissed her, reminded her to ring her mother later, and went back down to the car, waving as he drove off.

'Your stepdad's obviously fond of you,' commented Sam as he took the suitcases inside.

'He is, luckily for me,' said Hester affectionately. 'He's never had children of his own and tends to be protective where I'm concerned.'

Sam nodded in approval. 'Sounds like a good relationship. I'll just take this lot up to your room. Connah and Lowri stayed with Connah's mother over the weekend and they're not back yet, so you've got time to settle in before they arrive for lunch.'

'Talking of lunch, will you put this in the refrigerator for me?' Hester handed him a package. 'Or am I required to cook something hot?'

'Just soup and sandwiches, and Connah told me to stock you up for a cold meal tonight for supper.' Sam grinned. 'No need for a frontal assault on the cooker until tomorrow.'

'That's a relief! I brought a cold roast chicken just in case, but I can use some of that for sandwiches. After I've unpacked will you show me where everything's kept?'

'I'll give you a guided tour through the cupboards later,' promised Sam, and took her luggage upstairs.

Hester followed him, relieved that Sam Cooper seemed to like her. She unpacked rapidly and put her belongings away, then went downstairs to the kitchen. With Sam's guidance, she explored the cupboards and found them well stocked with everything she could possibly need.

'Has Connah lived here long?' she asked.

'No. The house was only finished properly a few weeks before we moved in. There was a hell of a lot to do. It dates from about eighteen-hundred and because it's a listed building it couldn't be hurried. Connah's main place is a penthouse flat in London but he's got business interests in this area, so when this house came on the market he snapped it up. Tomato is Lowri's favourite,' he added, as Hester surveyed the ranks of soup tins.

'Thank you. By the way, were there many other applicants for my job?'

'Three.'

But Connah had chosen her.

Sam answered her question before she asked it. 'Apparently the others were older and obviously set in their ways. Connah wanted a companion for Lowri, not a starchy, no-nonsense nanny.'

Hester began making sandwiches with the speed and efficiency of long practice. 'But officially I'm a housekeeper, not a nanny, remember.'

'Lowri will be glad of someone your age for company, whatever the job description,' Sam assured her. 'Normally she spends the holidays with her grandma at Bryn Derwen, but now Alice is married it's lonely there for her.' He munched appreciatively. 'These are first class.'

'I hope I haven't made them too soon.'

He shook his head. 'Connah said midday, so that's when he'll be here—' He broke off as his phone rang. 'Told you,' he said, checking the caller ID. 'Yes, Boss.' After a brief exchange, he disconnected. 'ETA twelve noon, Hester, and Lowri wants lunch in the garden. I'll help you take it out.'

Feeling far more nervous than before her interview with Connah, Hester put the soup to heat and prepared a tray.

'Lay for three,' said Sam. 'Connah expects you to join them for lunch.'

'Oh, right.' Hester hastily added a third setting. 'What does Lowri drink?'

'Fizzy stuff if allowed, milk or juice if not.'

'There wasn't time to make a pudding. Will ice cream do? Or fruit, maybe?'

Sam smiled reassuringly. 'Ask when you see her. Don't worry, Hester. She's a nice kid.'

Lowri's resemblance to her father was only slight. She showed promise of height like Connah's and her mouth was a smaller version of his, but her long straight hair was shades lighter and her eyes a striking cornflower blue.

'Hello,' she said, holding out her hand politely.

Hester took the hand. 'Nice to meet you.'

The bright eyes regarded Hester with frank curiosity. 'Daddy says you're going to look after us during the holidays. I thought you'd be like Mrs Powell, Grandma's housekeeper, but you're really young.'

Connah gave his daughter a warning look. 'Mind your manners, young lady. Remember what Grandma said. We must make Hester's stay here as pleasant as possible.'

'And I have to behave myself,' said Lowri, resigned, and gave him a smile so brimming with mischief that he laughed and gave her a hug.

'Hard work, I know, but you can do it.'

'Of course I can,' she said loftily, and beamed at Sam as he came into the kitchen. 'Did you bring my rucksack from the car?'

'It's in your room with the rest of your stuff.'

'Thanks, Sam.' She looked at Hester hopefully. 'I'm starving. Is it time for lunch soon?'

'Right away. Sam's already taken the tray into the garden, so if you go ahead I'll bring the food out.'

'You'll join us, of course,' said Connah courteously.

'Thank you.' Hester poured hot soup into a thermal jug, took the covered platter of sandwiches from the refrigerator and followed him into the garden.

Lowri polished off a bowl of soup with relish, despite the heat of the day, but Connah kept to sandwiches.

'Excellent chicken,' he commented. 'From the local delicatessen?'

Hester shook her head. 'I cooked it at home alongside my mother's Sunday roast. I wasn't sure what would be required for lunch today, so I made sure I had something ready.'

'You must let me reimburse you,' said Connah promptly.

'If you wish.' Hester smiled at Lowri. 'I asked Sam what you liked, so I put cheese and crispy bacon bits in some and just plain old ham in others. You can tell me what else you like as we go along.'

Lowri nodded, downing a sandwich at top speed. 'Yummy,' she said indistinctly, then shot a sparkling look at Hester. 'Though almost anything would be after school food.'

'Try the chicken, *cariad*,' advised Connah.

She made a face. 'They do that a lot in school.'

'Not like this,' he assured her, and with a martyred look Lowri took a minuscule bite.

Hester felt absurdly gratified when the blue eyes lit up.

'Wow! This is nothing like rubber school chicken. I *love* the stuffing.'

'How is your grandma?' asked Hester.

The blue eyes shadowed. 'She was very tired.'

'But getting stronger slowly,' Connah assured her.

Lowri gave her father a worried look. 'She doesn't look stronger. I didn't know she needed a nurse to look after her.'

'I insisted on hiring one for a while. At Grandma's age it takes time to get over surgery,' he told her. 'Don't worry. She'll soon pick up now she's beginning to eat normally again.'

'I hope so. Will she be well enough for us to have Christmas at Bryn Derwen?'

'Good Lord, yes.' He ruffled her hair. 'There's an entire term at school to get through before then.'

Lowri smiled as Sam approached with a coffee tray and a jug of orange juice. 'Is that for me?'

'Yes. Have you finished your lunch?' he demanded.

She smiled smugly at the empty platter. 'Every crumb.'

'No sarnies left for me?' he teased, then relented as she looked stricken. 'Only joking, pet. I ate mine before you arrived.'

'Did you have some with chicken?' she asked eagerly.

'I certainly did.' Sam put the tray down and bowed in Hester's direction. 'Best I've ever tasted.'

Connah finished his coffee and got up to follow Sam into the house. 'Thank you for lunch, Hester. Be good, Lowri; I'll see you ladies at dinner.'

Lowri heaved a sigh as she watched him go. 'Daddy's always so busy,' she said disconsolately. 'And he's got to go to London tomorrow. He said it's urgent or he wouldn't.'

'We'll have to think of things to do while he's away,' said Hester, pouring more juice.

'Thank you.' Lowri drank some of it, eyeing Hester over the glass. 'But won't you be too busy housekeeping?'

'No,' said Hester firmly. 'With Sam's help, it won't take long. The rest of the time I'll spend with you.'

Lowri gave her a very adult look. 'Will you tell me the truth?'

Help, thought Hester. 'I'll try. What do you want to know?'

'Are you really a housekeeper, and not some kind of nanny?'

'Hey, do I look like Mary Poppins?' Hester demanded, resorting to indignation to avoid a direct lie.

'No. But you don't look like a housekeeper either.' Lowri giggled, then sighed gustily. 'Anyway, Mary Poppins had two children to look after, and I'm only one. I'd just love to have a baby sister—even a baby brother would do.'

'Maybe that will happen one day.'

'I don't think so,' Lowri said forlornly, then brightened. 'But I've made lots of friends in school.'

'That's good. Your father says you really like it there.'

'I don't like all the lessons, but otherwise it's great. Some girls get homesick, but I don't.'

Because you don't have a mother, thought Hester with compassion. 'Right, I must get these things indoors. Would you carry the jug, please?'

Once the kitchen was tidy, Hester said it was time to unpack.

Lowri made a face. 'The trunk will be a mess. I'm rubbish at packing.'

'Then let's attack it right away. You can tell me where to put everything.'

'I don't really know. I've only been here once, and that wasn't to sleep,' said Lowri. 'I usually go back to Grandma's for school holidays, but last half-term I went to stay with Chloe Martin. It was brilliant. She's got two brothers and a little sister and her mother's very nice.'

'Is her father nice too?' asked Hester as they went upstairs together.

'Oh, yes, but I didn't see him much. He's in the police. A deputy something.'

No wonder Lowri was allowed to stay there. 'Deputy Chief Constable?'

'That's right.' The child scowled at the trunk beside her bed. 'I just hate this part.' She looked guilty as Hester raised the lid. 'I've got some clean things in my backpack, but it's all got a bit jumbled in here.' She sighed. 'If you *were* Mary Poppins you could make everything fly into the drawers.'

'Since I'm not, you can hang the things up from your back-pack and I'll take this lot down to be washed. Your blazer and skirt must go to the dry cleaners.' Hester cast an assessing eye at the tall, slender child. 'But I think you need new ones. You've grown out of these.'

'Yes!' Lowri punched the air in triumph. 'How soon can we go shopping? I want new jeans, lots of tops, trainers, a miniskirt like Chloe's—'

'Hold on,' said Hester, laughing. 'I need a chat with your father first.'

Hester loaded the washing machine then suggested they take a stroll in Victoria Park, but, with Connah's instructions fresh in her mind, she asked Sam to drive them there.

'I'll wait here, Hester,' he said as he parked near the entrance gates. He took a paperback thriller from the glove compartment. 'I'm well prepared.'

'Are you sure about this, Sam?' asked Hester.

'If you mean is it OK with the boss, yes. Just press my button and I'll come after you at the double if you need me. Not,' he added, looking round the peaceful, sunlit park, 'that I think you will.'

'I don't either.' She smiled wryly. 'But I'd rather not break any rules on my first day.'

Hester's previous charges had all been toddlers with limited conversation and it was a refreshing change to listen to Lowri talk about her friends in school and the boy from the farm near her grandmother's home.

'I used to go there to buy eggs with Alice—she was my nanny when I was little. Owen's twelve, but he's only a bit taller than me,' she said with satisfaction. 'He's nice. He helps on the farm after school and his father pays him wages. I just get pocket money.' Lowri looked at Hester hopefully. 'I've got some left. I could treat you to an ice cream from the park café. May I?'

'I don't see why not. I'll have a vanilla cone, please.'

Lowri's long legs covered the short distance to the café at top speed.

'Thank you,' said Hester, accepting her ice cream. 'Do you want to walk or sit while we eat these?'

'Walk, please!' Lowri cast Hester a glance as she licked. 'Do you live here in the town?'

'When I'm not working in other people's houses, yes. I have a flat all to myself at my stepfather's home.'

'One of my friends has a stepfather and she doesn't like him.'

'How sad for her! I'm lucky. Robert's a darling. He had my flat redecorated just for me. If your father agrees,' Hester added, 'I could take you to see it one day, if you like.'

Lowri's eyes widened. 'Go to your house? *Could* I?'

'We'll ask your father this evening. If he gives permission, I'll get my mother to make cakes. She's a great cook.'

'I hope Daddy says yes,' said Lowri wistfully. 'I never go to other people's houses, except to play with Owen sometimes.'

'You stayed with your friend Chloe,' Hester reminded her.

'Only because Grandma was too ill to have me for half-term.'

As they strolled back to the car, Hester hoped she hadn't raised hopes that Connah Carey Jones would dash. But he'd not only met her mother, he had good reason to be grateful to her. His daughter would come to no harm in the Marshall household.

As soon as they got back, Hester provided Lowri with milk and biscuits, then took a tea tray up to the study.

Connah looked up at her in surprise. 'Hester! Sam could have done this.'

'I'm supposed to be the housekeeper,' she reminded him. 'Lowri chose the biscuits, so please eat one or two.'

He stared down at the plate, bemused. 'Oh. Right. Thank you.'

'If you can spare a few minutes, I'd like to talk to you later,' she informed him.

'Problems?' he said sharply.

'None at all, so far. But I need instructions. You're obviously busy right now, so perhaps you'll let me know when it's convenient.' She smiled politely and went from the room, closing the door behind her.

She found Lowri glued to a cooking programme on the kitchen television, and Sam got up to go, eyeing Hester with something like diffidence. 'I eat my dinner downstairs on my own in peace, by the way.'

'Then I'll make a plate up for you. Any dislikes?'

'You serve it, I'll eat it,' he assured her. 'Thanks, that would be great, Hester. Connah eats at seven when Lowri's with him, so I'll collect mine a few minutes beforehand, if that suits.'

'Of course. I'll ring down when it's ready.'

Lowri tore her eyes away from the television when he'd gone. 'This programme's making me hungry.'

'Then let's see what's on the menu for dinner,' said Hester and went off to the giant refrigerator to find that Sam had ordered every conceivable kind of food necessary to serve a cold supper.

'Can we have more of your chicken?' said Lowri eagerly.

'We certainly can. I'll lay the dining room table.'

'Can't we eat here?'

Hester shook her head. 'I'm sure your father would prefer the dining room.' At least she hoped he would, then, like Sam, she could relax with her own meal in peace.

'I'll ask him!' Lowri shot out of the room before Hester could stop her and went running from the kitchen to make for the study.

Hester thought about following her to apologise, then shrugged. If Connah disapproved he could tell her in private later. She collected some potatoes and had scraped several by the time Lowri came back, tongue between her teeth as she concentrated on the tray she was carrying.

'Daddy said he only uses the dining room for visitors, and would you please put supper in here for the three of us.'

So that was another question answered. 'Thank you, Lowri. And before we eat we must have a bath and change our clothes.' Sometimes one just had to be nanny. 'But first I'll finish these potatoes, then wash some salad greens and boil some eggs. I'll show you how to devil them, if you like.'

Lowri nodded eagerly. 'Chloe's mother let us help her in the kitchen and make scones and things, but Mrs Powell does Grandma's cooking and she hates mess, so I don't go in the kitchen much in Bryn Derwen.'

'We'll do some baking some time, if you like,' offered Hester. 'And if you make a mess, you clean it up. Deal?'

'Deal!' said Lowri, beaming.

Sam had departed, with grateful thanks for his appetising meal, and Hester was decanting buttered, herb-scattered potatoes into a serving dish when Connah came into the kitchen in jeans and open-necked shirt, his hair still damp from a shower. And looked so much more like the man who'd taken her breath ten years ago that Hester's pulse went into overdrive as the scent of warm, clean male skin stood every hormone she possessed to attention.

'You look nice, Daddy,' said Lowri, running to him.

'Thank you, *cariad*, so do you.' He gave her a hug, smiling at Hester over the shining dark head of his child. 'Good evening.' He cast an eye over the dishes on the table. 'Tempting display.'

Get a grip, she ordered herself fiercely. 'Thank you. Lowri helped prepare it.' She smiled as the child launched into the list of things she'd done for the meal, including laying the table and devilling the eggs.

'You mash the yolks with butter and pepper sauce, Daddy,' she informed him. 'They're yummy.'

'I'm sure they are. And such a splendid feast deserves some wine,' Connah told her. 'Would you fetch three wineglasses from the cupboard over there? You can have lemonade in yours, and Hester and I will drink some New Zealand white.'

She certainly knew exactly where she stood with Connah Carey Jones, thought Hester as they sat down to the meal. But thank God he had no idea that she'd ever carried a torch for him—and still did, heaven help her.

'Hester said I can do some baking with her some time,' said Lowri, as she helped herself to potatoes.

'Brave Hester,' her father said dryly.

'Oh, it's all right, Daddy,' Lowri assured him. 'If I make a mess, Hester said I just clear it up afterwards.'

Connah smiled across at Hester with respect. 'An excellent policy.'

Lowri chattered nineteen to the dozen while they ate, but even so Hester found it hard to relax in the company of her new employer, who might still have the same effect on her hormones, but was nevertheless very different from the man she'd romanticised in her teenage dreams. However courteous and polite he might be, these days there was a remote, untouchable quality about Connah Carey Jones that only warmed when he was interacting with his daughter. As a result, Hester ate sparingly and, though she enjoyed the intense fruit flavour of the wine, refused a second glass when Connah offered it, and could see he approved.

'Tomorrow I'll make a pudding,' she said, as she began clearing away their empty plates. 'But tonight it's a choice of fruit or cheese.'

'I think Lowri's full, for once in her life,' said Connah, 'and I'll forgo the cheese in favour of coffee.'

'Certainly. I'll bring a tray up to you.'

'Better still, I'll wait while you make the coffee, then take it up myself,' said Connah firmly.

Hester thanked him and switched on the coffee-maker, glad that it was a make she was familiar with, since she had an audience for the process.

'When the coffee's ready, Lowri, we'll leave Hester in peace for a while,' said Connah. 'How about a game of chess?'

She nodded fervently. 'Can you play chess, Hester?'

'I can, but sadly I'm out of practice.' She turned to smile at the child. 'You can bring me up to speed on a rainy day some time.'

'Incidentally, Hester,' said Connah, 'I like Lowri to be in bed by nine normally, but she can have an extension tonight. Put a glass of milk on the tray, then she'll be ready for bed when you come to fetch her.'

'Hester made me drink milk at teatime. Do I have to drink it again?' complained Lowri.

He ruffled her hair. 'Yes, you do.'

Hester heaved a sigh of relief when they'd gone, envying Sam his solitary dinner. It was a draining experience to spend time in Connah's company without betraying by the flicker of an eyelash how much it affected her. She glanced at the clock, found she had almost an hour's grace, and got to work. When the kitchen was tidy, Hester went up to her room to make repairs to her face, then sat down in the buttoned velvet armchair by the window to do absolutely nothing for a few minutes, well aware that at seventeen she would have been on cloud nine at the mere thought of living in the same house as the man of her dreams. Especially a house like this one. Neither of her previous jobs had provided her with such appealing private quarters.

Unlike Lowri's, which had pink flowers trailing down the wallpaper and a hammock suspended over the bed to house the soft toys she'd brought with her, Hester's room had cinnamon walls and carpet and white curtains and bedcover, all of it brand-

new, including a writing desk and a combination television and
DVD player. Everything was bound to be new, of course, if the
house had only just been redecorated, or restored, or whatever.
Doing up a listed house of this age had to be a huge undertak-
ing. At the mere thought of the permits required, Hester yawned
widely, wishing she could just crawl into the tempting brass bed.
With a sigh, she got up, tucked her white shirt into her narrow
black skirt, then went downstairs to knock on the study door.

Lowri opened it, smiling all over her face. 'I'm beating
Daddy,' she said with triumph, pulling Hester over to the desk.

Connah looked up from the chessboard with a wry smile.
'You've snatched me from the jaws of defeat, Hester.'

'You haven't lost yet,' Lowri comforted him. 'We can go on
with the game when you get back and maybe you'll win in the end.'

She obviously thought this so unlikely that Connah laughed.
'Off to bed with you, champ. Give me a kiss.'

Lowri threw her arms round his neck and he pulled her on to
his knee to kiss her.

'Goodnight, Daddy.'

'Goodnight, *cariad*, sleep well.' He stood up and set her on
her feet. 'I'll be off early in the morning, Hester, so if you need
to speak to me, see Lowri settled then come back down.'

CHAPTER THREE

WHEN Hester went downstairs again Connah motioned her to one of the sofas facing each other across the fireplace.

'Did Lowri settle down happily?'

'Yes. She was tired enough to welcome going to bed.'

'It's been a long day for her,' agreed Connah and sat opposite, eyeing her closely. 'So, Hester, Lowri seems to have taken to you. Do you think you'll enjoy spending time with her?'

'I will, very much. She's a delightful child—remarkably adult in some ways, yet still a little girl in others.' Hester smiled. 'Up to now I've worked with under-fives, so it's quite a revelation to be with someone of Lowri's age. There was one sticky moment, though,' she added. 'She asked me point-blank if I was a nanny.'

He raised an eyebrow. 'And how did you answer?'

'To avoid the direct lie, I asked—very indignantly—if I looked like Mary Poppins.' Hester gave him a straight look. 'But if she brings it up again I prefer not to lie.'

'She probably won't. It's just that Alice—her former nanny—was never required to cook meals.' He paused. 'Thank you again for dinner. I normally eat out or have it sent in. But I don't expect you to cook for all of us on a regular basis.'

'I have no problem with that. I like cooking. I'm no cordon bleu chef, but my mother's a very good cook and taught me well. And Lowri likes helping in the kitchen so it's a good way of keeping her occupied.'

'And will do her in good stead when she has to fend for herself one day. Thank you, Hester. I'll adjust your salary, of course.' He eyed her expectantly. 'So what did you want to talk about?'

'First on the list, clothes. Before I take Lowri shopping, I need a clear idea of what you want—and don't want—for her.'

Connah looked taken aback. 'I thought you'd know more about that than me.'

Hester smiled. 'For starters, she wants jeans, tops and trainers and—I warn you—a miniskirt like Chloe's.'

He laughed. 'Then buy her one. She'll look cute in it.' He gave her an impersonal, assessing look. 'Judging by your taste in clothes, she's in good hands.'

Hester felt a warm sensation inside at his comment on her appearance. 'Thank you. The list is pretty extensive. When I unpacked her trunk I found that Lowri's outgrown practically everything, including her uniform.'

Connah got up to go over to the desk. 'I order that through the school. I'll give you the number and you can get on to that right away. They add it to the bill for fees.' He came back with a thick roll of notes. 'For shopping here in town I'd rather you used cash, Hester.'

'As you wish. I'll keep a list of what I spend.' She paused. 'Talking of clothes, I dressed soberly today, for obvious reasons. But for walks and picnics and so on I'd be more comfortable in something casual, if you're happy with that.'

'Wear what you like,' he said, surprised. 'In fact, the less you dress like a nanny the better.'

'Thank you.' She looked at him in appeal. 'Now I have a favour to ask. Could I have your permission to take Lowri home to see my mother one day? When I broached the subject, Lowri was very enthusiastic.'

For a moment Hester was sure that he was going to refuse point-blank. Then he smiled wearily. 'I must seem like an ogre to you, keeping my child shut away from the world.'

'I'm sure you have good reason.'

'I do. But Lowri would enjoy a visit to your home. I remember your mother very well.' His eyes softened. 'Is she up to entertaining a lively ten-year-old?'

'She'll just love it. So will Robert, my stepfather. You can check with Sam about him, if you like. They met when Robert insisted on delivering me here this morning.'

'I already have. Your family was cleared when John ran the security check on you.' Connah got up to cross to a drinks tray. 'Have a nightcap before you go up, Hester.'

'I won't, thank you.' She got up, battening down her resentment. 'I'll look in on Lowri, then take myself to bed.'

'In that case, I'll say goodnight.' He walked with her to the door. 'I won't see you in the morning, but if you need to speak to me at any time while I'm away, Sam will know where to find me.'

'Thank you. Goodnight.'

'Goodnight, Hester.'

She forced herself to walk slowly upstairs instead of running up to burn off some of her annoyance. Connah Carey Jones might be paying her well for her services but he was getting good value for every penny. She was an experienced, highly qualified nanny, who could also cook and keep house. And, as the icing on the cake, her family had unknowingly passed John Austin's security check with flying colours. It was the unknowing part that really hacked her off, no matter what her hormones felt about him.

Lowri was fast asleep. Hester drew the covers higher and went to her own room to ring her mother to report on her first day in the Carey Jones household. Moira was full of eager questions, which Hester answered in detail before mentioning the proposed visit with Lowri. This received such an enthusiastic response that Hester promised to bring the child round for tea as soon as possible.

'We've got some shopping to do first, Ma. Lowri needs clothes, and I must have a session at the supermarket.'

'Come on Wednesday afternoon, then. I'll bake.'

'I told Lowri you would!'

Hester woke next morning at six as usual, and got up to shower before Lowri surfaced. Leaving the sleeping child to the luxury of a lie-in, Hester went silently downstairs to the kitchen to make herself a cup of tea, and almost turned tail and went out again when she found Connah there before her, drinking coffee, dressed ready to leave and looking so much the embodiment of every dream she'd ever had that Hester was struck dumb for a moment.

'Good morning, Hester,' he said, surprised. 'You're an early riser.'

She pulled herself together, irritated by the effect he had on her. It was too much to cope with at this time of day. 'Good morning. Babies and toddlers wake early, so it's a habit I can't break. Lowri is still asleep, so I left her in peace for a while.'

He gave her one of his piercingly direct looks. 'Actually I'm pleased to have caught you before leaving. Last night I could tell that you were unhappy about having your family investigated, Hester, but where Lowri is concerned you must appreciate that I can't take risks.'

'And now you know that my stepfather is a recently retired headmaster and my mother the daughter of a clergyman, you'll be happy to leave Lowri in my care,' she said without inflection, and moved past him to fill the kettle.

'From your point of view, I was sure of that the moment I saw you with John at the Chesterton,' he said, surprising her.

She swung round in surprise. 'You were there when he interviewed me?'

'Beforehand, not during. I sat outside in the lounge behind a newspaper.' He shrugged. 'I was beginning to despair by the time you arrived. The other three might have been suitable carers for small babies, I suppose, but much too old to be a companion for Lowri.'

'So my age was your main reason for employing me?'

'It was part of it, yes.' He gave her a sudden disarming smile. 'But watching you talk to John as he saw you out, I knew Lowri would take to you. And, to be candid, I'm sure the others would have marched off in high dudgeon if asked to pose as my housekeeper.'

'But you thought I'd take it in my stride?'

'I think you take most things in your stride, Hester.'

She smiled a little. 'After years of looking after other people's children, I should have the knack by now.'

Connah smiled back as he put his empty cup in the sink. 'Am I forgiven for the security check?'

When he smiled like that she could forgive him anything. 'I expected one for myself as a matter of course. But no one's ever checked up on my family before.'

'Will you do me a great favour?' he asked, surprising her.

'If I can,' she said cautiously.

'I assume that your mother knows I'm the man who came knocking on her door in the snow all those years ago?'

'Of course. I rushed home to tell her after the first interview—' Hester halted. 'By the way, if you saw me at the Chesterton, may I ask why you interviewed me twice?'

'The first time was to make sure that my first impression was right, and you were exactly what I was looking for. But I had to wait for the security check before I could call you back to offer you the job.'

'I see.' She held the look steadily. 'So what favour do you need?'

'Have you told your family I had them investigated?'

'Certainly not.'

'Good. In that case, could you keep it to yourself? Your stepfather would probably just be furious, but your mother would be hurt. I don't want that any more than you do, Hester.'

'Then I won't tell her.' She glanced at the clock. 'Can I cook you some breakfast?'

'Coals of fire?' Connah smiled crookedly. 'It's a tempting thought, but no, thanks. I must be on my way. If you need to speak to me while I'm away, ring me.'

'I hope I won't.'

'I know you do,' he said, and left her to her tea.

'Good morning,' said Sam, coming into the kitchen a few minutes later. 'Did you see the boss before he left?'

'Yes, I did. Good morning, Sam.' She finished her tea. 'There's more in the pot if you want. I'd better check on Lowri. She was out for the count when I got up.'

Hester smiled wryly as she went up to Lowri. The job had an unexpected benefit. Three flights of stairs would do wonders for her personal fitness.

Lowri was still out for the count. Hester eyed the sleeping face for a moment, then scribbled a note to ask Lowri to come down for breakfast when she woke. With the radio for company, Hester had ironed half the contents of the trunk by the time the yawning child finally trailed into the kitchen in her dressing gown.

'Good morning,' said Hester, smiling. 'How about scrambled eggs?'

Lowri nodded sleepily. 'Yes, please.' She slid into a chair at the table, watching as Hester folded the ironing board. 'Has Daddy gone?'

'Yes, he left very early.'

'Do you know when he's coming back?'

'He didn't say.' Hester poured orange juice into Lowri's glass. 'But cheer up. He said yes to a visit to my mother and Robert.'

Lowri's face lit up like a Christmas tree. 'When? Today?'

'No, tomorrow for tea. Today we go shopping for clothes.

Then we have some lunch and shop for food. How's that for a programme?'

'At last!' said Lowri when Hester emerged from her own room later in a navy cotton shirt and white denim skirt. 'You look nice. Can I buzz Sam now and say we're ready to go?'

The morning was tiring but very entertaining. Let loose in a shopping mall packed with chain stores full of clothes that sent her into raptures, Lowri looked through every last bit of merchandise in each shop they went into, it seemed to Hester, before she made her final choices. But though Connah had handed over a generous sum of money, Hester firmly steered her charge past shops that sold expensive designer clothes.

'You'll be tired of them or have grown out of them, long before you get your money's worth,' she said practically. 'And with those long legs everything will look good on you, anyway. With shoes it's different, no economising there.'

'Trainers?' said Lowri hopefully.

'Of course. And something less sporty too.'

'Not school shoes!'

'No. At least not yet. We leave those until the end of the holiday.'

They loaded their packages on to a patient Sam, then made for a café to wait while he stowed everything in the car.

Not sure of the protocol, Hester was relieved to hear that Sam had always lunched with Lowri and Alice during shopping trips near Bryn Derwen.

'But Alice is married now, to Owen's father,' said Lowri as she downed her drink thirstily. 'Owen's mother died when he was little, and his grandma brought him up, just like me. But she's got arthritis now, so Mr Griffiths married Alice.'

'That's nice for Owen,' said Hester.

Lowri nodded sagely. 'Alice used to take me to the farm a lot, so Owen's known her for ages. He thinks she's cool. It's a very good arrangement, Grandma says.'

Not least for Mr Griffiths, thought Hester, and looked up with a smile as Sam came in to join them.

'Good,' said Lowri. 'Let's eat!'

When Hester finally got to bed that night she stretched out with a sigh of relief, confident that she'd made a reasonable start with Lowri. There'd been an awkward moment at suppertime when the child had wanted Sam to stay and eat his lasagna in the kitchen with them, but he'd refused, saying he liked to read the paper while he ate his dinner and, in any case, he couldn't leave the monitors that long.

'You leave them when you come out with us,' Lowri had pointed out mutinously, but he told her that was different and he had to get going or his dinner would be cold.

It was different, Hester could have told Lowri, because when he was out with them, Sam had Lowri under his watchful eye all the time. Here in the house, his job was to keep unwanted visitors away for the same reason. But Hester also had an idea that Sam refused to cross a line he saw as clearly defined. Connah thought a great deal of Sam Cooper, it was obvious, but the relationship on both sides was still very much employer and valued employee. And, since Connah had elected to dine in the kitchen when he was at home, it would have been awkward if Lowri had expected Sam to join them.

We'd have made an ill-assorted quartet, thought Hester wryly. In her former job, the question of eating with her employers had never arisen. They were both successful actors with working hours that varied according to the film or television series they were involved in. It was Hester who'd made the children's supper. The three-year-old Herrick twins, Sebastian and Viola, were engaging children Hester had been very fond of. But when their parents won lead roles in an American television series, nothing they could say would persuade Hester to accompany the family to Los Angeles.

Hester sighed as she stared through the window at the stars. After a job in a theatrical household, her next post would be very different. George Rutherford, her new employer, owned a very successful haulage firm. His wife Sarah was still helping him run it, seven months into her first pregnancy at the age of forty-one, and had every intention of going back to work after the birth, leaving Hester very literally holding the baby.

But, before all that, Hester reminded herself, she had six weeks in Connah Carey Jones's home, which was not only a dream come true on one level, but a very pleasant way of earning some money before she moved on to pastures new. One of the downsides to her job was parting with her charges when the time came. She sighed in the darkness. She'd known Lowri for only a very short time, but she already knew that it would be no easier to part with her after six weeks than it had been with the other children after several years. And this time there would also be the painful wrench of parting with Lowri's father.

CHAPTER FOUR

HESTER'S phone jolted her awake next morning.

'Connah here. Good morning.'

Heart thumping for various reasons, not least the sound of his voice, she took a deep breath. 'Hello. Is something wrong?'

'A bad case of guilt. I had a totally manic day yesterday. By the time I had a moment free, it was too late to ring either Lowri or you. Was she upset?'

'If she was she didn't say so. She had a wonderful day. After the shopping spree, she was quite sleepy after supper and settled down in bed shortly after nine. Shall I get her for you now?'

'No, don't wake her. When she gets up, tell her I apologise. Was the shopping trip a success?'

'Very much so. Brace yourself for an itemised—and very long—list of her new clothes when you see her. I'm taking her to tea with my mother this afternoon, by the way.'

'I only wish I could gatecrash the party. Please give your mother my regards.'

'I will. Goodbye.'

Hester snapped her phone shut and slid out of bed to make for the bathroom. Half an hour later she looked in on a deeply sleeping Lowri and went down to the kitchen to enjoy a peaceful—and very early—breakfast. It had been a mistake to tell Connah she was an early riser. If it hadn't been for his phone call, she could have stayed in bed a little longer for once. And, more importantly, without the fright of thinking something was wrong at home.

After a late breakfast Lowri spent a happy hour sending texts to friends on her treasured phone, while Hester saw to the minimal duties necessary to preserve the fiction that she was a housekeeper before she took her charge off to the park for some exercise.

Lowri was all for it, provided she could wear her new combat trousers. 'Perfect for a run,' she announced, doing a twirl for Sam in the kitchen.

This time, rather to Hester's surprise, Sam elected to accompany them into the park. 'I like a run myself now and then,' he announced.

Lowri eyed him doubtfully. 'I run fast,' she warned.

'Run a bit slower today then, so Sam can keep up,' said Hester, giving him a sly grin.

When they got back to the house later, Sam went down to his own quarters to make himself some lunch and Hester and Lowri ate alone.

'Just one sandwich,' said Hester. 'We must leave room for my mother's tea.'

'It must be lovely having a mother,' sighed Lowri. 'Or even a stepmother like Alice. Owen's so lucky.'

'Did you see them over the weekend?'

'Yes. Daddy took me down to the farm to get eggs, and we all had tea and fruitcake. Alice baked it. She asked Owen's grandma for the recipe.'

Good move, Alice, approved Hester.

Lowri was ready well before time to leave in a new denim mini-skirt and pink T-shirt to match her new pink and white trainers.

'How do I look?' she asked Sam.

'Very grown-up!'

She smiled ecstatically. 'I can't wait to show Chloe my new things.'

Lowri's excitement visibly mounted as Hester gave Sam directions on the journey. When they reached the house Robert was waiting at the gate. He opened the rear door of the car and gave the passengers his gentle, irresistible smile.

'Hello. I'm Robert and you must be Lowri. Welcome.' He held out his hand to help her out and Lowri smiled back at him shyly.

'Hello. It's very nice of you to ask me to your house.'

Well done, thought Hester, and gave her stepfather a hug. 'Hi, Robert. You've met Sam, of course.'

Sam shook hands, then asked Hester what time he should return to fetch them, but Robert shook his head.

'We insist you stay to tea, Sam. My wife has spent most of the day baking.'

Hester grinned. 'And she'll be mortally offended if you don't stay to eat some of it.'

Moira waved from the open doorway as they climbed the steep path to the house. She hugged her daughter, then turned to Lowri with a warm smile and held out her arms. 'Could I possibly have a hug from you too, darling?'

Lowri was only too happy to be hugged. Then she remembered her manners and introduced Sam, and Moira led the way through the house into the back garden, where tea was laid under a large umbrella on a table surrounded by a selection of odd garden chairs.

'What a lovely garden,' said Lowri rapturously. 'We've just got a sort of patio in the townhouse.'

'This must be hard work,' commented Sam with respect, and Robert nodded.

'But I enjoy gardening, and so, thank God, does my wife.'

'That's why he married me,' said Moira, exchanging a sparkling look with her husband. 'Now we'll leave you men to set the world to rights while we do the tea. Will you help me carry the food out, Lowri?'

'Yes, *please*!' She went into the house with Moira, chattering about devilled eggs and the baking she was going to do with Hester.

'That's one very happy little girl,' said Sam, watching, and Robert nodded, his eyes fond as they followed his wife.

'Moira has the knack of making people happy. I'm a fortunate man.'

How fortunate was soon demonstrated by the quantity of cakes and savoury delicacies covering the table.

'If you eat like this, how do you stay so fit, sir?' asked Sam, awed.

'A steep garden on several different levels takes care of that,' Robert assured him wryly. 'Besides, this is a special occasion, not everyday fare.'

The tea party was a great success. And since the adults took pains to include Lowri in the general conversation, her delight in the occasion was a pleasure to see.

'And now,' said Hester later, when they'd helped Moira clear away, 'I'll take you to see my own private lair, Lowri, but be careful on the steps.'

Lowri followed Hester up the open-tread iron staircase eagerly, her eyes round as they entered the flat. 'This is so *cool*! Is it just this one big room?'

'More or less. There's a small bathroom through that door at the end.'

'It's perfect,' sighed Lowri rapturously. 'I'd love a place of my own like this one day. Could I bring Daddy to see it?'

'Do you think he'd want to?' said Hester doubtfully, not sure she wanted Connah's overpoweringly male presence invading her private space.

'I want him to see what I'd like.'

'Time we went back to the others,' said Hester firmly. 'Careful on the stairs!'

It was late that evening before Lowri said her goodbyes and

thanked her hosts very prettily for having her. 'I've had such a lovely time.'

'So have we. You must come again soon, darling,' said Moira, and handed Lowri a large box. 'I've put a few cakes in there for your tea tomorrow.'

'Oh, *thank* you!' Lowri reached up spontaneously and kissed Moira's cheek, at which point Robert demanded a kiss too.

'Right then, folks,' said Hester. 'I'll give you a ring later in the week. Thank you for this.'

'My thanks also,' said Sam. 'It was an unexpected treat, and much appreciated.'

When they were in the car on the way back into town, Lowri heaved a great sigh. 'What a darling house. It must be so lovely to live there, Hester.'

'It is, but actually I'm not there very much. In my kind of job I live in the house where I'm—employed. I don't get home here nearly as often as I'd like.'

'You must get very homesick.'

'I miss my mother, certainly.'

To Hester's dismay, tears suddenly slid down Lowri's flushed cheeks. 'If I had a mummy like yours I would too,' she said, so forlornly that Hester put an arm round the child and held her close in wordless comfort all the way home.

It was so late by the time they arrived that Lowri was only too happy to go straight to bed. She fell asleep so quickly that Hester turned off the DVD player, left a night light on and went down to the kitchen. If Connah wanted to talk to his daughter tonight he was out of luck. But, as she sat down at the table with the daily paper and a mug of tea, it dawned on Hester that, unlike Lowri, a sandwich and one of her mother's cakes had been her entire food intake for the day.

Hester toasted two slices of sourdough bread, spread them

with butter and marmalade and sat down to enjoy her snack while she caught up on the day's news. She was making a second pot of tea later when she heard footsteps on the stone stairs leading up from the basement and turned with a smile, expecting Sam. Her heart gave a deafening thump when Connah strolled into the kitchen instead, smudges of fatigue under eyes which lit with such involuntary pleasure at the sight of her that Hester sat, transfixed.

'Hello,' she said at last, breaking the spell.

'Good evening, Hester,' he said, clearing his throat, and dumped down his briefcase. 'Sam thought you'd gone to bed.'

'Not yet. Though Lowri's asleep,' she said, getting a grip. She gestured towards the teapot. 'I've just made a fresh pot. Would you like some tea?'

He slung his jacket on the back of a chair and sat down at the table. 'I had my sights set on a shot or two of whisky, but now you've mentioned it I think maybe I would like some tea. First, anyway.'

'I didn't realise you were coming back today,' said Hester, shaken by her delight at his unexpected appearance.

Connah raked a weary hand through his hair. 'When I spoke to you this morning it wasn't on the agenda. But things went better than I expected, so I thought why the hell am I going back to a lonely flat tonight when I can be home with my daughter in a couple of hours?' He smiled. 'Of course Lowri's asleep now, but at least I'll be with her first thing in the morning.'

'She'll be thrilled. Have you had dinner? I could cook you something.'

'I had a cholesterol-heavy lunch, so thanks for the kind thought but I won't trouble you to cook tonight, Hester.' He eyed her expectantly. 'Maybe you could rustle up a biscuit or two?'

'Of course.' She opened the box containing her mother's cakes. 'Or perhaps you'd like one or two of these.' She put a selection on a plate and put it in front of him. 'My mother sent them home with Lowri.'

Connah bit into an almond tart with enthusiasm. 'Delicious,' he said indistinctly. 'So how did the tea party go?'

'Huge success.' Hester smiled. 'But I'll let Lowri tell you all about it tomorrow. I had a job to tear her away—it was late when we left.'

'I hope your mother wasn't too exhausted!'

'She enjoyed it enormously, so did Robert. Sam, too, by the way,' she added. 'He was all for depositing us there and collecting us later, but my parents wouldn't hear of it.'

'Knowing your mother even as little as I do, I can well believe that.' He shrugged. 'I suppose I should have made things clearer for you from the start where Sam is concerned, Hester, but his role in the household is somewhat hard to define.'

'It's not a problem because Sam himself is totally clear about it. So he joined us for lunch on the shopping trip, and for tea today, but dines alone—in peace as he puts it—in his own quarters.' Hester looked at him levelly. 'I was quite prepared to do the same, until you instructed otherwise.'

He stared. 'It's utterly pointless for you to eat alone in here, while Lowri and I dine in solitary splendour in the dining room—which is the only room in the house I dislike, by the way. You might take a look at it tomorrow and tell me where I went wrong.'

Not sure she would dare to do that, Hester sat down with her own tea. 'Did you use an interior designer?'

'Originally, yes, but the woman had ideas so bizarrely different from mine we soon parted company. The study, the dining room and the master suite are down to me. Your room too,' he added, 'which is why it's a touch stark.'

'Not to me. It's exactly to my taste.'

'Good. By the way, did you apologise to Lowri for me?'

'Yes, but I didn't say you'd ring in case something prevented that.' She eyed him thoughtfully. 'She was a bit blue on the way home tonight.'

He frowned. 'Why?'

'Seeing me with my mother emphasized the lack of one herself.' In for a penny, in for a pound, thought Hester. 'She would like a baby sister. Even a baby brother would do.'

Connah stared, thunderstruck. 'She told you that?'

'Oh, yes. She's madly envious of her friend Owen because he's acquired a stepmother.' Hester's lips twitched. 'Be warned. She'd like one of those too.'

'Good God!' He held out his cup for more tea, looking poleaxed. 'She's never said a word to me.'

'It's woman to woman stuff. Please don't let on that I told you.'

'I won't, but I'm glad you warned me. I try to give her most things she wants, but in this case she'll just have to deal with disappointment.'

Influenced by the intimacy of the situation and the lateness of the hour, Hester found herself asking a question so personal she regretted it the moment it was out of her mouth. 'You have no plans to marry again?'

She held her breath, certain that Connah would tell her it was nothing to do with the woman he was employing to look after his daughter, but, to her immense relief, he merely shook his head.

'Not even for Lowri will I marry just to provide her with a stepmother, Hester. She'll have to find something else to wish for.' His mouth turned down. 'But at the weekend my mother informed me that Alice is expecting a baby, so in view of what you've just told me I suppose I can expect fireworks from Lowri when she hears that piece of news. Apparently Owen doesn't know yet, but I doubt that a boy of his age will be thrilled.'

'He might be if Lowri envies him.'

'True.' Connah eyed the empty plate in surprise. 'I seem to have eaten all the cakes.'

'There's plenty more in the box. Are you sure you wouldn't like me to cook you something?'

He shook his head and got up with gratifying reluctance. 'I'd better take myself off to the study for some of that whisky I mentioned.' He gave her the smile that had bowled her over when she was seventeen and was doing pretty much the same right now, all the more potent because it was the first time she'd witnessed it at full power since then. 'You must be desperate to get to bed. Tomorrow I'll get something sent in for once to give you the evening off. And I'll put Lowri to bed myself,' he added, collecting his briefcase. 'Don't mention that I'm home when she wakes in the morning. I want to surprise her.'

'Of course. Goodnight.'

Hester cleared away, then went straight upstairs to check on Lowri. Later, armed with a paperback thriller her mother had given her, she settled down in bed in a glow of well-being which soon faded when she traced it not only to Connah's return but because he'd seemed as pleased to see her as she was to see him. She sighed. This was something to be nipped in the bud right now. He was a very different man from the mysterious Mr Jones who'd set her teenage pulse fluttering. But, although he still had much the same effect on her ten years on, no way was she getting involved again with someone related to a child in her care.

Lowri was utterly delighted when Connah walked into the kitchen during breakfast next morning.

'Daddy! I didn't know you were home,' she cried, jumping up to hug him.

'I came late last night and asked Hester not to tell you so I could give you a surprise,' he said, taking her on his knee. He kissed her and smiled down into the sparkling eyes. 'You're getting so big I won't be able to do this much longer. I won't have room on my lap.'

She beamed up at him. 'Did Hester tell you what a great time I had at her house yesterday?'

'Not yet; she said you'd want to tell me yourself.'

'Before Lowri starts on her saga,' said Hester quickly, 'what would you like for breakfast?'

Connah smiled at her warmly. 'Oh, just toast and coffee, please.'

While Lowri launched into her account of the tea party, Hester made a pot of coffee, poured orange juice, filled a silver rack with wholemeal toast and put it all on the tray she'd laid ready for the breakfast Sam had told her Connah ate in the study while he caught up with world news and the state of the stock market. Hester took the tray upstairs and left it on the desk, but Connah frowned as he came into the room with Lowri. 'I could have brought that up myself, but thank you, Hester.'

'Not at all. It's my job. Lowri can tell me when you've finished.'

'I was just telling Daddy about your flat, Hester,' said the child eagerly. 'I can't wait for him to see it.'

'We can't intrude on Hester's home, *cariad*,' Connah told her, and gave Hester a questioning look.

'You're welcome to any time,' she said casually. 'Not that there's much to see.' She left father and daughter together and went back to the kitchen to make herself a cup of coffee she could drink in peace on her own. She wondered why Connah had objected when she's taken his breakfast up to the study. After all, it was what housekeepers did. Or would he have preferred Sam to do it, as presumably he'd done before she arrived on the scene? If the appropriate moment presented itself, she would ask to save further embarrassment. It presented itself sooner than expected when Lowri came to tell her that her father had finished his breakfast.

'He wouldn't let me bring the tray down myself,' she said crossly.

'Only because he didn't want you to slip on those stone stairs and hurt yourself,' said Hester briskly. 'Now, you think about what you'd like to do today while I fetch it.'

Connah turned from his computer screen as Hester knocked on the study door. 'Come in. Sit down.'

She took the chair in front of the desk and looked at him warily.

'Lowri may be unaware of your true role in this house, but I am not,' said Connah bluntly. 'Which means I don't expect you to fetch and carry for *me*, Hester.'

'You obviously prefer Sam to do it.'

He frowned. 'I wouldn't put it that way exactly; I just think he should. You were engaged to look after Lowri, not wait on me. The fact that you also cook for us is more than enough.'

'As you wish,' she said, feeling rebuffed, and got up. 'But I'll take the tray since I'm here.'

All through the day, while she was making lunch and walking with Lowri in the park, Hester found herself wondering why Connah's edict had annoyed her. Any Norland-trained nanny worth her salt should have been glad that he refused to have her wait on him. But she felt hurt that he didn't want her in and out of his study on a regular basis. The rapport of the night before had obviously been a figment of her imagination.

'What's the matter, Hester?' asked Lowri, eyeing her anxiously.

'Nothing, why?'

'You were frowning.'

'The sun's strong today.'

'I know. I'm hot! Can I buy us some ice creams again, please?'

'Of course.' Hester fished in her purse for change. 'Only this time let's sit down to eat them.'

'OK.' Lowri ran off to the café, but before Hester could find an empty bench she spotted a man speaking to Lowri and raced towards them, pressing the button on her phone for Sam as she went, by which time Lowri was in possession of two ice cream cones and the man was nowhere to be seen.

'Who was that man, Lowri?' gasped Hester, her heart in her throat.

'I don't know. He wanted to buy me an ice cream.' Lowri grinned at Hester's look of outrage as she handed one to her. 'Don't worry, I said no, thank you—very politely—and he went away. It's all right,' she added soothingly, 'that kind of thing's hammered into us in school.'

'What kind of thing?' demanded Hester.

'Never to talk to strangers, and never, ever, let them sell you anything or buy anything for you.'

'So you know the drill. Good,' said Hester, fighting for calm. 'What did the man say?'

'He asked if you were my mother—wow, Sam's in a hurry,' Lowri added as he sprinted to join them.

'What's up?' he demanded, and Hester explained while Lowri demolished her ice cream.

'Before we go back to the car,' said Sam, his eyes hard, 'how about we take a walk through the park, Lowri? If you see the man, point him out to us.'

She shrugged. 'I didn't take much notice of him, Sam. But he had smart clothes. He was rather nice.'

'What's the matter?' Hester asked, as Lowri sighed heavily.

'I suppose you'll stick to me like glue from now on.'

'You'd better believe it!'

The child's mouth drooped. 'If you tell Daddy, you won't have to—he won't even let me come in the park any more.'

Or sack the nanny on the spot.

But Connah was surprisingly calm when Hester reported the incident the minute they got home. 'Did you know the man?'

'No.'

'Would you know him again?'

'I doubt it. I took one look, and ran to break it up. But he'd disappeared by the time I reached them. I do apologise. I'll know better another time.' Hester looked at him squarely. 'If there's to be another time. For me, I mean.'

'Of course there will,' he said, surprised. 'My daughter's become attached to you so quickly there'd be hell to pay if I tried to replace you.'

'And I to her,' Hester assured him. 'In the circumstances, perhaps Sam could take us further afield for our walk tomorrow.'

'Good idea. Take a picnic lunch.' Connah's eyes softened slightly. 'Relax, Hester. There was no actual harm done.'

She sighed. 'I suppose not. But in future I'll be doubly vigilant.'

Connah Carey Jones took so long to get his daughter to bed that night, he felt respect for Hester and for Alice before her, who, like his mother, managed the process so effortlessly. When it became obvious that Lowri was drawing it out to see how far she could go before he lost patience, he kissed her one last time and told her to go to sleep, or else.

'Or else what, Daddy?' she said, smiling at him.

'Try it and find out,' he growled, and Lowri, knowing she'd pushed the envelope far enough, blew him a kiss and settled down.

Connah smiled to himself as he closed the door. Lowri was growing up fast. The thought gave him a sharp pang as he went downstairs. All too soon she would be a teenager, with all the problems that entailed. Problems he would have to deal with single-handed.

As he passed the lower landing window, he caught sight of Hester's graceful, athletic figure coming into view and stood still, watching her walk towards the house, suddenly aware of how empty it had felt without her for a few hours. He raised a sardonic eyebrow. Empty, with Lowri and Sam in residence? Lacking, then, rather than empty. After only a matter of days, Miss Hester Ward had become a vitally necessary part of life in Albany Square. To him, he admitted, as well as to Lowri. Which was preposterous in such a short time. But a fact, just the same. He wanted more of Hester's company than just at mealtimes with Lowri, or a few minutes when the child was in bed. With sudden decision he thought of the ideal way to achieve it, then his eyes narrowed as he saw Hester pause at the foot of the steps to speak to a man who'd been following her along the pavement. Connah craned his neck, but the man was just out of view. After a moment or two Hester ran up the steps to ring the bell and he hurried downstairs to intercept her as she made for the kitchen.

'You're home early,' he commented.

She smiled at him. 'There's a film on television I missed at the cinema, so I left after supper to walk back in good time. Robert wanted to drive me, but I felt like the exercise—always a good move after one of my mother's little suppers.'

'I saw you from the landing window,' Connah informed her.

'You were watching for me?' The dark blue eyes frosted over. 'Am I late?'

'Of course not. I happened to be passing the landing window when I noticed a man following you. Was he someone you know?'

'No. Just someone asking directions to Chester Gardens,' she said coolly, and went past him into the kitchen.

'If you're making coffee, I'd like some too,' he said, feeling wrong-footed as he made the request. She was in his employ, dammit. He had the right to ask her to make him a cup of coffee. His jaw set as she promptly laid a tray with a solitary cup and saucer. 'I want your company while you drink it,' he informed her crisply.

Hester looked at him for a long moment, then nodded. 'Very well.'

'Put another cup on the tray and come up to the study with me. Please. I want to talk something over with you.'

Connah took the tray from Hester and waved her ahead of him up the stairs.

'Is it something about Lowri?' she asked, then regretted it. What else could it possibly be?

'Actually, it's about Sam. Sit down, Hester.' Connah put the tray down and sat on the sofa opposite to watch her pour. 'He's long overdue for a holiday. If he knew Lowri was safe with me, Sam might agree to take a few days off.'

Her face cleared. 'In which case, I could make sure she didn't disturb you when you were working, if that's your problem.'

'It's not.' Connah gave her a searching look. 'Hester, had you ever seen the man before?'

'Which man?'

'The one asking directions just now.'

She tensed as she saw where this was leading. 'You think it might have been the man in the park?'

'Do you?'

Hester gave it some thought. 'I honestly don't know. I only saw him fleetingly. He was gone by the time I reached Lowri.'

'Describe the man tonight.'

'Tallish, slim, well-dressed, about your age, maybe—' She put her coffee down untouched. 'He *could* have been the same man, but I can't swear to it.'

'You probably think I'm paranoid on this subject, but I dislike coincidences.' Connah drained his cup and sat back. 'Let's go back to Sam's time off.'

Hester shook her head. 'If Sam feels the same about coincidences, he'll refuse point-blank to take any.'

'I know, so I won't bring it up.' Connah gave her a very direct look as he played his trump card. 'But if you and I take Lowri on holiday, Hester, we'll be well away from this mystery man, whoever he is, and Sam could enjoy some R and R with no worries. Lowri would be delighted,' he added. And her father could spend a great deal more time in Hester's company than was feasible in Albany Square.

She returned the look steadily, wondering if he realised how much the idea appealed. 'Do you normally take Lowri away during her summer vacation?'

'Yes. My mother comes with us.'

'But I was a complete stranger until a few days ago,' she pointed out, playing devil's advocate. 'Are you sure you want me along? Wouldn't you prefer to be on your own with Lowri?'

Connah shook his head. 'Lowri wouldn't go unless you came too, Hester. You were the main topic of conversation tonight.'

'How boring for you,' she said lightly. 'More coffee?'

'Thank you.' Connah sat back with his refilled cup, his eyes on Hester's face. 'So will you come?'

Of course she would. Anywhere. 'Do you have somewhere in mind?'

'Italy. A friend of mine owns a villa in Chianti country in Tuscany. I'll have a chat with him and hope by some miracle that the house is free for a couple of weeks. It's a picturesque place, with terraced gardens and a pool with a view. Lowri would love it.'

Me too, thought Hester. After the South of France fiasco, a holiday in Tuscany with Connah and Lowri was the stuff of dreams. 'It sounds idyllic.'

'Then you agree,' Connah said with satisfaction. 'You own a current passport?'

'Of course. Does Lowri know about this?'

He shook his head. 'I consulted you first. No point in getting her hopes up if you refused to come.'

As if! 'You engaged me to work for you for six weeks,' said Hester, smiling, 'but you didn't specify where, so I have no right to refuse—even if I wanted to, which I don't. Thank you. I'd love to come.'

'Good. That's settled, then. I'll talk to Jay.' Connah got up and went over to the drinks tray. 'How about a nightcap first?'

Hester got up quickly. 'I won't, thanks.'

He swung round to face her. 'Of course, I forgot. You rushed back to see a film.'

'Yes,' she agreed. 'I can still catch most of it.'

Connah walked to the door and opened it for her. 'Goodnight, Hester. Not a word to Lowri in the morning about the holiday, in case it doesn't come off. And if it does I'd like to break the glad news to her myself.'

'Of course. Goodnight.' Hester went slowly up to her room, wishing she could have stayed talking to Connah for a while. But she was attracted to him so strongly it was getting harder and harder to hide the fact from him. And because he also paid her salary it was necessary to keep to a strictly professional level of employer and employee between them. Not that Connah had the least idea that she thought of their relationship in any other light. And resisting the temptation of a tête-à-tête with him at this time of the night had been one way of making sure he kept thinking that way.

CHAPTER FIVE

LOWRI was so enraptured with the idea of a holiday which included Hester, she talked non-stop over the breakfast her father shared with her at the kitchen table for once to tell her that his friend, Jay Anderson, was happy for them to stay at his villa in Tuscany, not just for a fortnight but for a whole month.

Four whole weeks, thought Hester.

'Can Hester take me shopping again before we go, Daddy?' Lowri demanded, after a pause to draw breath.

He smiled and ruffled her hair. 'You didn't buy enough clothes last time?'

'Hester didn't buy me a new swimming costume!'

'How remiss of you, Hester,' said Connah dryly. 'In that case, you two can raid the shops again today with Sam while I take a trip to Bryn Derwen to tell my mother what's happening.'

Lowri looked worried. 'Shouldn't I go too?'

'Not this time. We'll visit her when we get back.'

'Hester too, so I can take her to see Alice and Owen.'

Connah ruffled his daughter's hair. 'After a holiday chasing after you in Tuscany. Hester will be glad of a break. Besides,' he added, 'she'll want to visit her own mother as soon as she gets back from Italy.'

Which could mean that he didn't want her to visit his, thought

Hester, trying not to feel hurt. 'Then when you get back from Grandma's, Lowri,' she said briskly, 'we'll be busy getting you ready for school before I leave.'

Lowri's face fell. 'Then I suppose you'll be someone else's housekeeper.'

Hester avoided Connah's eyes. 'I have another job to go to, yes.'

'Where is your next post, Hester?' asked Connah.

'Yorkshire.'

Lowri's mouth drooped. 'Is that too far to come home on your day off?'

'I'm afraid so,' said Hester with regret.

Lowri brightened. 'But when you come home to see your mother and Robert, couldn't you do it at half-term? Then you could see me too.'

'You'll be spending next half-term with your grandma,' Hester reminded her.

'True,' said Connah, and got up. 'But you're welcome to visit Lowri there any time you fancy a trip into Wales during the school holiday, Hester.'

She thanked him politely, sure that this was merely a courtesy to soothe his disconsolate daughter. 'I'll just clear away, then we'll get ready to go shopping, Lowri.'

'And I,' said Connah, pulling his daughter to her feet to hug her, 'must be off on my travels to get to Bryn Derwen in time for lunch.'

'Are you coming home again today?' demanded Lowri.

'Yes,' he assured her, 'but not before your bedtime. If you're asleep, I'll see you in the morning. Now, give me a kiss, then you run upstairs and tidy your room while Hester finishes down here.'

'OK. Give Grandma a big kiss for me.'

When the child had gone, Connah gave Hester a wry smile. 'She's grown very attached to you.'

'It's mutual,' admitted Hester, shutting the dishwasher. 'This is the hardest part of my job. It's so painful to say goodbye to the children I care for.'

He watched her in silence for a while as she moved round the room, putting things away. 'Have you never thought of having children of your own?' he asked at last.

She shot him a startled look. 'Of course, but only in the abstract.'

His eyes glinted. 'By which I take it you've never met someone you consider suitable to father these children?'

Hester's chin tilted. 'That's a very cold way to look at it.'

'Ah! You mean you'd have to be in love with the prospective father first.'

'He would have to be someone I cared for, certainly,' she said stiffly. 'And vice versa. It makes for security for the child. You should understand that. You're a very loving father.'

He sobered. 'The loving part is easy, but I have to function as both parents to Lowri, which is difficult sometimes. So tell me, Hester, do I shape up to the other fathers you've met in your line of work?'

'Admirably.' Hester gave the counters an unnecessary sponge-down. Something about Connah in his present mood was unsettling.

'You've never asked me about Lowri's mother.' Connah's eyes took on an absent look, as though he was gazing far back into the past. 'When she died I felt as though half of me had died with her and I never want to feel that way again.'

Hester stared at him, aghast, shocked that he should tell her something so intensely private.

He looked at his watch, suddenly very much back in the present. 'I'm late. I'll call in on Sam on the way down to the garage and tell him to shape up for another shopping session with Lowri. He has the Bryn Derwen number if you need to contact me.'

Why couldn't she be trusted with the number herself? Hester smiled politely. 'Have a good trip. I hope you find your mother better.'

'Thank you. By the way, since this holiday is entirely my idea, please use some of the money I gave you for yourself.'

She shook her head. 'That's very kind of you, but I already have everything I need.'

'What an independent soul you are, Hester.' He gave her a mocking smile. 'See you tonight.'

Hester went upstairs to Lowri after Connah had gone, her mind still reeling—not only from shock about the revelation itself, but the fact that he'd confided something so personal to her. She wished he hadn't. The unexpected glimpse into Connah Carey Jones's private life left her with severe qualms about their next encounter.

Lowri's mood improved enormously once they were back at the shopping mall, though she was disappointed when Hester refused to buy a new swimsuit.

'I don't need one, Lowri. Honestly. Let's concentrate on you.'

'And this time,' said Sam firmly, 'I come in every last shop with you.'

'I hope you can keep up, then,' said Lowri, giving him a cheeky grin.

After a couple of hours of intensive shopping Sam took charge of the bags Lowri and Hester loaded on to him but, instead of taking them up to the car park, stayed with them when they went to look for lunch.

'Daddy told you to stick to us every minute, I suppose,' sighed Lowri, as she studied a menu in the café they chose.

'That's right,' agreed Sam cheerfully. 'Now, what shall we eat?'

'I'll order a salad, then pop into the pharmacy over there while you choose yours,' said Hester. 'I forgot to buy more sunblock.'

'We'll stay put then, Lowri,' said Sam, and gave Hester a straight look. 'Don't be long.'

Leaving her companions wrangling about their choices, Hester walked swiftly across the mall to make her purchases.

When she hurried from the shop afterwards she collided with a man who apologised profusely as he picked up the packages she'd dropped.

'Did I hurt you?' he demanded.

'Not in the least,' she said firmly, taking her parcels.

'Let me buy you a cup of coffee to make amends.'

'No, thank you. I have someone waiting for me.'

'Of course you have,' he said with regret and, when she pointedly waited for him to go, he gave her a wry little salute and walked away.

Hester gazed after him with narrowed eyes. She wished she could have taken him up on his offer so Sam could vet him. Because she was pretty sure he was the man who'd asked for directions in Albany Square, and therefore possibly the man in the park as well. But she couldn't risk letting him anywhere near Lowri. She hurried back to the café to find Sam and Lowri making inroads into their lunch.

'A good thing you ordered a salad,' said Sam. 'We wondered where you were.'

'Sorry, folks. The shop was busy. Is your pizza good, Miss Jones?'

Lowri nodded with enthusiasm. 'It's yummy! Sam said it was all right to start or it would get cold.'

'Of course. I'm ready for mine too.'

When they got back to the house, Hester sent Lowri up to her room with some of the bags and told Sam about the incident, which was assuming alarming proportions in retrospect.

'I thought something was up when you took so long,' he said grimly. 'You'd recognise him again, then?'

'Yes.' Hester frowned. 'Odd thing—there's something familiar about him.'

'Bound to be if you saw him last night.'

'No. Other than that. Yet I'm sure I've never met him before.'

'Could he be the guy in the park?'

'Possibly. But I wouldn't swear to it.' She grimaced. 'Shall I tell Connah or will you?'

'Your shout, Hester. You actually saw him, so you can give him a proper description.'

'Or the entire thing could be a coincidence.'

Sam looked her in the eye. 'I don't believe in coincidences.'

'Neither does Connah,' she said glumly, and picked up the rest of the shopping. 'You'll be glad when we're safely on our way. Are you going somewhere exciting?'

Sam laughed. 'My mother used to say that her idea of a holiday was for my dad and me to go away and leave her in peace for a week, and now I see what she means. So when you three go I'll stay put, Hester, to make sure nothing goes amiss with this place. I'll have a nice little holiday with nothing to do but answer the door, keep my phone charged and take down any messages. A few DVDs, a good book or two and a list of numbers to phone for whatever cuisine takes my fancy—what more can a man ask?'

'Company?'

'The occasional pint down the pub will take care of that.' He patted her hand. 'You enjoy yourself in Italy with Lowri and the boss. I'll be fine.'

Hester's worries about feeling awkward with Connah were unnecessary. He arrived home earlier than expected, his manner matter-of-fact as he announced that he was so hot after the long drive he fancied eating supper outside on the patio.

'It's a beautiful evening. Can you do something cold, Hester? Or I could get a meal sent in—'

'I've got the makings for a Caesar salad, if you'd like that.'

'Sounds good to me.'

'How was your mother?'

'She's not recuperating nearly as rapidly as I'd like,' he said, frowning. 'It's going to take time and patience before she's back to normal. Where's Lowri?'

'She was a bit tired and hot after our shopping trip, so she had a bath and said she fancied watching television in the study. As of five minutes ago, she was still doing that.'

'I'll go and see her, then take off for a shower.' Connah smiled at her. 'What an efficient creature you are, Hester. Nothing seems to throw you off balance.'

He was wrong there, she thought grimly. He'd done that very effectively just this morning. And the incident with the stranger in the shopping mall had made it twice in one day. But Connah could learn about that later, when Lowri was asleep.

The treat of supper in the garden was welcomed with great enthusiasm by Lowri.

'It's just like a picnic,' she said happily, when her father sent her down to the kitchen, 'only we've got a proper meal instead of sandwiches. I'll help you carry things while Daddy's in the shower, Hester.'

'Thank you. If you'll ring down for Sam, he can come to collect his meal before we take the salads out.'

When Sam arrived he put the supper Hester had ready for him in the refrigerator. 'Before I eat I'll take whatever you want out to the patio.'

With Sam and Lowri helping it was a simple matter for Hester to get a meal ready in minutes on the marble table under the vines. The only task left for Connah, when he appeared a few minutes after Sam went downstairs with his own meal, was to open the bottle of white wine keeping cool in an ice bucket in the shade.

Connah removed the cork, filled two glasses, poured lemonade for his daughter and sank down with a sigh of pleasure at the table. 'This is just what I need. We'll be able to eat outside all the time at Casa Girasole.'

'Even breakfast?' said Lowri, eyes shining.

'Even breakfast,' Connah agreed. 'But I hope you bought plenty of sun cream today. There'll be no venturing outside without it once we get there, young lady.'

'Hester bought extra while Sam and I were waiting for our lunch,' Lowri informed him.

'Of course she did,' said Connah, smiling at Hester, and helped himself to the salad. 'So how many bathing suits did you buy, Lowri?'

'Only three, Daddy. A plain blue one, and a really cool yellow bikini, and a sort of top with little matching shorts.'

'You must show them to me later. How about you, Hester?' added Connah. 'Was sun cream your only purchase?'

'No, indeed. I also bought a floppy white hat, two paperback novels and topped up my first aid box.'

'So we are now prepared for all eventualities,' he said, smiling at her. 'Excellent salad, by the way. Just the thing for an evening like this.'

'Thank you.' She put some on her plate. 'After supper I'd like to visit my mother, if that's all right with you. I need to collect some things from my flat.'

'Of course.'

'Can I come?' said Lowri eagerly, then sighed mutinously when her father shook his head.

'Let Hester have a quiet hour with her mother.'

'I'll take you there when we come back,' promised Hester. 'Then you can tell my mother and Robert all about your Italian holiday. They went there for their honeymoon four years ago, so they'll enjoy that.'

'Only four years ago?' said Lowri, diverted. 'I thought they'd been married for ages.' She thought about it. 'Do older people have honeymoons when they get married, then?'

'Certainly,' said Connah. 'Alice did when she married Mal Griffiths, remember.'

Lowri nodded. 'They went to Paris on the Eurostar. Alice bought me a silver Eiffel Tower charm for my bracelet.'

Hester smiled at her. 'Robert took my mother off to Italy for a month.'

'If they were away that long you must have missed them an awful lot,' said Lowri with sympathy.

'Not really, because I was working. Though I had time off for their wedding, of course, which was a lovely, happy occasion. I was their bridesmaid.'

The blue eyes widened. 'Really? Did you have one of those puffy dresses with a big skirt?'

'Afraid not,' said Hester apologetically. 'Mine was short and quite plain, but it *was* silk.'

'Have you got pictures?'

'Of course. I'll bring some back with me tonight.'

'Talking of which,' said Connah, 'leave all this, Hester. Give Sam a buzz. He can drive you to your parents' home.'

'No need. It's a lovely evening. I can walk—'

'No, Hester,' he said with finality. 'Sam will give you a lift. He can fetch you again later.'

And much as she wanted to protest, Hester gave in rather than upset Lowri by arguing.

'Though this wasn't necessary,' she told Sam on the short journey.

'If this joker's on the watch for you, it might be,' he reminded her. 'And, although it could be just your big blue eyes that draw him, Hester, if he's the man in the park it's likely he sees you as a way of getting to Lowri.'

Hester eyed him with horror. 'To kidnap her?'

'Or he could just be a paedophile attracted to *her* big blue eyes. Either way, it's not going to happen if I can help it. So I'll drop you at the garden gate, then come back an hour later. In the meantime, I'll clear your supper things from the patio.'

'Sam, you're a star!'

'I know.' He gave her a sidelong grin. 'Don't worry. Connah pays me well.'

Hester eyed his profile thoughtfully as they reached the house, wondering what regiment he'd been in. 'Thank you, Sam. See you in an hour, then.'

Hester found Moira and Robert sitting at the table in the garden with glasses of wine. They were delighted to see her, but surprised when Hester told them she was off to Italy with Lowri and her father for a whole month.

'This is a bit sudden, darling,' said her mother.

'Connah's idea. I could have rung you, but I thought it better to come and see you instead.'

'Much better,' said Robert. 'Have a drink. We opened a very nice red for dinner.'

'Yes, please. Will you shudder if I ask for lemonade in it?'

'You can have whatever you want,' said Robert, and went into the house to fetch it.

'Are you looking forward to the trip?' said Moira, eyeing her thoughtfully.

Hester nodded. 'Of course. I took Lowri shopping for bathing suits today. She's very excited.'

'She's a delightful little girl. Our Mr Jones has done very well with her.'

'True, but he's had his mother's invaluable help until recently. She's taking a long time to recover from heart surgery, poor lady. Which, of course, is why I'm looking after Lowri. And a trip to Tuscany's not to be sneezed at. I'll be able to send you postcards from some of the places you visited.' She grinned at Robert as he came back with the lemonade. 'Lowri was surprised to hear you and Mother had a honeymoon, by the way.'

He chuckled. 'Thought we were too old, of course,' he said, and kissed his wife's hand.

'I promised to take her the wedding pictures,' said Hester. 'Could you dig them out while I round up my holiday gear from the flat?'

'Drink your wine first,' said Moira. 'Relax for a while and let us enjoy your company, darling, while we can.'

Hester smiled and sat back. 'Right. So tell me what you've both been up to lately.'

'Gardening,' they said in laughing unison.

The time flew by as Hester sat, relaxed, in the cool of the evening. In the end it was an effort to heave herself out of her chair to go up to her flat to collect the clothes bought for the French holiday that never was. When she was carrying her suitcase down the steps from the flat later, she stopped dead as she heard a new male voice. Connah, not Sam, had come to drive her back to Albany Square. And it was pointless to deny that she was utterly delighted about it.

CHAPTER SIX

CONNAH crossed the lawn to take Hester's suitcase. 'Sam is playing chess with Lowri,' he informed her, smiling. 'So, because I'm spiriting you out of the country, I came to renew my acquaintance with your mother and introduce myself to your stepfather at the same time.'

'Come and sit down, Hester,' said Moira. 'Connah's having a drink before driving you back.'

'Tonic only,' he assured her.

Hester sat down and let Robert refill her glass, knocked off her stride for the third time that day. 'This is a surprise,' she remarked.

'I came to assure your parents that I'll take good care of you in Italy,' he said smoothly.

'And we're very pleased you did.' Moira smiled warmly at Connah. 'I'm so glad to see you again. I thought about you such a lot after your stay with us.'

'I've never forgotten how kind you were,' he said sombrely, then changed the subject and turned to Robert. 'Is this garden all your work, sir?'

'No, indeed. My lady wife works as hard as I do.'

'And I've got the hands to prove it,' said Moira, holding them up. 'You have a delightful daughter, by the way, Mr—I mean Connah.' She smiled wryly. 'I confess I still tend to think of you as our mysterious Mr Jones.'

He grinned and glanced at Hester. 'You, too?'

'At first, but I grew out of it,' she lied, flushing. 'By the way, Mother, Lowri would like to visit you and Robert again when we come back, to tell you about her travels.'

'We'll look forward to that,' said Robert, and patted his wife's hand. 'Just give Moira a couple of hours' notice to make cakes.'

'My daughter never stops talking about the wonderful time she had here,' said Connah. 'She keeps telling me she's set her heart on a flat of her own like Hester's one day.'

'I know,' said Moira, laughing. 'She wanted you to come and see it. So now you're here you may as well. Robert's rather proud of it because he did the decorating himself.'

'In that case I can hardly leave without taking a look,' said Connah promptly. 'With your permission, of course, Hester.'

'Come this way,' she said, resigned, and led the way across the garden and up the steps. 'As I told you, there's not much to see.'

Connah followed her into the long, uncluttered space, filling it, just as she'd feared, with his dominant male presence. 'I can see why you feel at home in your room in Albany Square,' he commented after a while. 'This is remarkably similar.'

'I'm very lucky to have it,' Hester assured him, annoyed because she sounded breathless. 'I chose the paint and the furniture while I was here for a weekend, and next time I came home, here it was, beautifully decorated by Robert and ready for occupation. Mother put up a couple of watercolours from my old room at home, and insisted on buying a few cushions to make this one look less spartan, but otherwise it's all my own taste.'

'I can see why Lowri likes it so much.' Connah smiled wryly. 'On the other hand, if you'd gone for carpet and wallpaper awash with cabbage roses she'd probably feel the same, just because it's yours, Hester. She thinks the world of you.'

'And I of her.' Which was worrying, because in a few weeks' time they'd have to part.

'You can always come back and visit her in the future,' he said softly, reading her mind, and held her eyes. 'Your welcome would be warm, I promise.'

Hester controlled the urge to back away. 'Thank you. But now I'd better get back to put Lowri to bed.'

The drive home was achieved in silence which neither broke until Connah turned into the private road behind the house in Albany Square.

'You thought I was intruding tonight, Hester?' he asked abruptly.

'Of course not. Mother was delighted to meet you again.'

'I had the feeling you were not.'

'I was surprised,' she said sedately, as the car glided into place beside Sam's in the garage. 'I was expecting Sam.'

'Would you have preferred that?' he questioned hastily.

Hester eyed him in surprise as she got out of the car. 'Not particularly.' Her eyes narrowed. 'You disapprove of fraternisation among the hired help?'

Connah threw back his head and laughed. 'So there is some fire inside that cool shell. Come off it, Hester. You don't look on yourself and Sam as hired help any more than I do. To me, Sam is both friend and employee, while you—' he paused, thinking it over '—I'm not sure how to categorise you, exactly. I find it difficult to think of you as either nanny or housekeeper.'

She eyed him in alarm. 'You mean my work isn't satisfactory?'

'God, no, quite the reverse.' Connah leaned on the roof of his car, eyeing her across it. 'You take good care of my child, you cook well and you're not only easy to look at, I'm very comfortable in your company. The hard part is thinking of you as an employee.'

'Nevertheless, I am,' she said matter-of-factly, 'and right now I must do what you pay me for and put your daughter to bed.' She turned as he followed her up the stairs to Sam's level. 'Once she's settled for the night, I need to talk to you.'

'Why do I get worried when you say that, Hester?' he said,

sighing. 'All right. Do what you have to do, then come down and have a drink. And this time don't say no. Serious discussion goes better over a glass of wine.'

Lowri's reception was so warm that Connah laughed as he reminded the child she'd been parted from Hester for only hours, not weeks.

'It seemed like a long time. And I would have so liked to go with Hester to see her mother and Robert,' said Lowri, sighing heavily.

'They sent their love, and said they look forward to seeing you when you get back. And while you're at the villa perhaps you'd like to send them postcards of the local scenery to show where you are,' said Hester, and smiled at Connah. 'Thank you for the lift.'

'My pleasure. Goodnight, sleep tight, Lowri.'

'Goodnight, Daddy.' Lowri gave him a careless wave and slipped her hand into Hester's. 'Will you watch some television with me for a while? It's early yet.'

'It's not early, young lady,' said her father, 'but Hester can stay with you for half an hour after she takes you up. But then you must get to sleep or you'll be too tired to travel tomorrow.'

Lowri brightened and jumped to her feet, full of questions about Hester's parents as they made for the door.

'Half an hour,' called Connah. 'Then I need Hester myself.'

His choice of words had an unsettling effect that Hester couldn't get rid of as she sat on her usual chair by Lowri's bed to show her the wedding photographs she'd brought. Of course Connah hadn't meant the words literally. But it would be good to be needed by someone like him as a woman, instead of as someone suitable to look after his daughter. Not just good—wonderful. And as much a fantasy as any of the dreams she'd woven about him when she was seventeen. Hester shook herself out of her reverie when she saw Lowri had fallen asleep.

She went downstairs to knock on the study door and found

Connah reading the *Financial Times*, a half empty glass on the table in front of him. He got up with a smile and went to the drinks tray.

'What will you have, Hester?'

'Tonic water, please. Lowri fell asleep quite quickly, by the way.'

'No prizes for guessing why. Once you were there to settle her down, she was fine.' Connah poured the drink, added ice and slices of lime and handed it to her, his eyes sombre. 'She's going to take it hard when you leave us.'

'She'll soon adjust when she's back in school. She likes it there, she told me.'

'Yes, thank God. Now sit down and tell me why you need to speak to me.'

Hester described the incident outside the pharmacy. 'It was the same man who asked directions the other night.'

'Was it, by God?' Connah's face set in grim lines. 'What did you do?'

'I refused his help politely and stood my ground until he moved off. I would have liked Sam to get a look at him, but I couldn't risk letting him anywhere near Lowri.'

'Maybe it was quite innocent and the man was just trying to pick you up,' said Connah and smiled, his eyes gleaming. 'Who could blame him?'

She flushed. 'Possibly. But he looked familiar, which worried me. Though I'm sure I'd never seen him before the other night, unless he is the man in the park. I didn't get a good enough look that day to be able to tell.'

'But if you met this one again, you'd recognise him?'

'Definitely. I was so pointed about not moving until he did, I had time for a good look at his face, also of his back view as he walked away. He was wearing casual clothes, but they were the expensive, designer kind, like his shoes. And he wore a Rolex watch,' added Hester.

Connah gazed at her with respect. 'You're very observant.'

'In this case only because I thought it was necessary. I doubt I'd have noticed any of that in ordinary circumstances.' She gave him a worried look. 'I'm really glad we're going away tomorrow. Whoever this man is, we'll be out of his reach.'

'Which was part of my reason for organising the holiday.' Connah finished his drink, then sat back. 'Right then, Hester, with that thought in mind, I want you to forget about the man and relax while we're away. The house is a mile or so from the village, so there aren't many people around to bother us. It has a private pool, a maid to do the housework and shopping, so you have nothing to do except keep Lowri entertained. No small task, as I know to my cost, even though you make it look easy.'

'In my last post I looked after three-year-old twins,' she reminded him. 'After my stint with Seb and Viola, sweet children though they are, taking care of Lowri is a breeze.'

'A theatrical household must have been interesting,' he commented, leaning back.

'It was.'

'Did you meet many famous thespians?'

'One or two, yes. But Leo and Julia, the twins' parents, were on stage in different theatres during the last few months I was there, so I spent most of my time with only the twins for company.'

'Quite a responsibility.'

'True,' agreed Hester, 'but it's what I was trained for. I was in at the deep end right from the start of my first job. I had to complete nine months of satisfactory work with the children of the first family who engaged me before I could actually qualify as a Norland-trained nanny.'

'Which you did, of course, though I can't remember your CV in detail. Were you with the first people long?'

'Three years, until the family went to Australia. Beforehand they had recommended me to their friend, Julia Herrick, and I went straight to Julia a month before she gave birth to the twins.'

'And when you leave us you're going off to Yorkshire,' said Connah, his eyes sombre. 'I'm already dreading the day you part with Lowri.'

So was Hester. 'As I said before, it's the part of my job I don't enjoy.' She finished her drink and stood up. 'But now I'd better finish packing.'

Lowri was fast asleep, with her head on Hester's shoulder, missing the incredible views as Connah drove along the final stage of their journey on the Chiantigiana, the famous road that meandered through the hills and vineyards of Tuscany. The air-conditioning in the car was fighting a losing battle with the heat of the day and Hester felt hot and weary by the time they were in sight of the sleepy little village they were heading for. To her disappointment, Connah turned off without entering it and took a narrow, stony road that curved up through umbrella pines and ranks of tall cypresses towards high pink walls at the top of a hill.

'Is that Casa Girasole?'

'It certainly is.'

Connah nosed the car through high wrought iron gates and drew up in the courtyard of a pink-washed house with Juliet balconies at the upper windows. Hester gazed in delight, drinking in heat and sun and flowers growing in profusion in rich hot earth. Tiny pink roses twined in the greenery, curling round the pillars of the loggia, and three descending tiers of flower beds held drifts of white jasmine among scarlet and pink geraniums and the cheery faces of the sunflowers that gave the house its name.

He turned round in his seat to smile at Hester. 'Well?'

'It's absolutely lovely,' she said softly, and Lowri stirred and sat up, rubbing eyes which suddenly opened wide in delight.

'Are we here? Is that the house? Gosh, it's pretty! Why didn't you wake me?'

'You're awake now,' said her father, and got out to open the passenger door. 'Out you get. Hester must be squashed and very hot. You started snoring on her shoulder as soon as we left Florence.'

'I don't snore!' said Lowri indignantly, then her eyes lit up as she spotted a blue glint in the distance. 'Wow! Is that the pool? Can we have a swim before supper?'

'After you've unpacked, yes.' Connah helped Hester out of the car. 'First we find Flavia, otherwise we can't get in.'

'*Signore!*' Right on cue, a plump young woman came hurrying round the corner of the house and let out a cry of delight as she saw Lowri. No translation was needed for her flow of liquid welcome as she expressed her pleasure to see them. Shooing them before her like a hen with chicks, she ushered them across the loggia into a living room with a shining terracotta tiled floor and furniture covered in sunny yellow chintz.

'What's she saying, Daddy?' demanded Lowri, smiling help-lessly in response to the lava-flow of conversation.

'We must sit and have drinks, while Flavia takes our luggage upstairs, only I'm not going to let her do that,' said Connah firmly and, with creditable fluency, told Flavia in her own tongue that refreshments would be welcome, but he himself would carry the bags up to the bedrooms.

'I'll carry my own,' said Hester at once, but Connah waved her away.

'For once, you will just sit there,' he said with such firmness that Lowri laughed.

'When Daddy talks like that you have to do as he says or he gets cross, Hester.'

'And you wouldn't want that, Hester, would you?' mocked Connah.

Hester smiled, defeated, secretly only too glad to subside on the sofa in the blessedly cool room.

Connah relieved Flavia of a huge tray and brought it to a glass-topped table in front of Hester.

'How do you say thank you, Daddy?' asked Lowri, her eye caught by a plate of little cakes.

'*Grazie*,' said Connor, and went out to unpack the car.

'*Grazie*, Flavia,' said Lowri, and the woman beamed, patted the child's hand and pointed to a teapot.

'*Tè*,' she said, then indicated the other pot and a tall jug clinking with ice. '*Caffè*, *limonata*.' Then, with a determined look on her face, she left the room to follow Connah.

'I think she's going to help with the luggage,' said Lowri, examining the rest of the tray. 'Daddy won't be cross with *her*.'

'No,' agreed Hester. 'I'm sure he won't.'

'Why are there two jugs of milk?'

'I expect one's hot for the coffee and the other's cold for tea.' Hester grinned as she heard sounds of altercation outside. 'Who do you think is winning?'

'Daddy always wins,' said Lowri positively, but for once she was wrong.

Connah came into the room later, looking unusually hot and bothered.

'Flavia insisted on helping you?' asked Hester, smiling.

He nodded ruefully. 'When I tried arguing, she pretended she couldn't understand me.'

'Have some coffee, Daddy,' consoled his daughter. 'I left you some cakes.'

'Thank you, *cariad*. What are you having, Hester?'

'Tea. And very welcome it is,' she said fervently, pouring coffee for him.

'Once we've recovered, we'll explore,' said Connah. 'Apparently Flavia normally leaves at five, but stayed later tonight to welcome us. She showed me the cold supper she left for us, and promises to cook whatever we want for lunch tomorrow.'

Lowri was thrilled with everything about the villa, from her airy bedroom next to Hester's to the big, bright kitchen big enough for three of them to eat meals at the table at one end, and outside the arcaded loggia with table and chairs for the outdoor meals her father had promised. But best of all were the beautiful terraced gardens, which led down in tiers to the crowning glory, an oval pool surrounded by well-tended grass and comfortable garden furniture with shady umbrellas and a view of Tuscan hills that begged to be photographed.

Connah smiled indulgently as he watched Lowri running about in delight to explore everything.

'Your friends have great taste,' commented Hester, impressed.

'And the money to indulge it. Jay Anderson was my partner until I sold him my share of the asset management firm we founded together. I still keep a stake in it, but these days I spend some of my time—and money—on restoration of properties like the house in Albany Square. I bought it with the intention of using it as my headquarters in the Midlands. But the house feels so much like home to me now that I'm not so sure I want to do that.'

'You could still use it for meetings,' suggested Hester. 'The dining room certainly feels like a boardroom, with all those chairs and that long table. Meals could easily be served there if you have business lunches.'

Connah eyed her with respect. 'You're right. The room could be a lot more useful that way than for dinner parties.'

'Can we have a swim?' demanded Lowri, running towards them. 'It's still lovely and warm.'

'What do you think, Hester?' asked Connah.

'Just for a few minutes, then. We'll unpack the swimming things, but afterwards we must hang up the rest of our clothes before we have supper.'

Lowri was ready to agree to anything as long as she could go in the pool, but Connah declined her invitation to join them.

'I,' he said virtuously, 'will go up to my aerie on the top floor and unpack, then have a shower. I shall join you later for supper.'

Hester was glad to hear it. Her swimsuit was the plain black one she'd worn to teach the twins to swim, and she'd long since lost the puppy fat of her first encounter with Connah. Nevertheless, she preferred to enjoy her first swim with just Lowri for company.

Lowri was out of her clothes and into her bathing suit at the speed of light and harried Hester to get ready quickly before it was too late.

'The pool will still be there tomorrow,' said Hester, laughing, as she collected towels.

The pool was set in natural stone and constructed with such skill that it looked as though it had always been there rather than man-made. The water was silken and warm on Hester's skin as she sat on the edge to dip her feet in it, and she smiled indulgently as Lowri jumped in with a terrific splash at the other end and swam towards her like a small torpedo. She stood up, waist deep, when she reached Hester, pushing her wet hair back from her beaming face.

'Isn't this *gorgeous*?' she gasped. 'I just love it here. Come on in. I'll race you to the other end.'

Lowri counted to three, then they set off for the far end, Hester careful not to overtake the child. They swam several lengths, then Hester called a halt as she saw Connah stroll up to watch them.

'Did you see us, Daddy?' said Lowri as she held up a hand. 'I think Hester let me beat her.'

Connah pulled her out, then held out a hand to Hester. 'You both looked far too energetic for me.' He handed a towel to Hester, then enveloped his daughter in the other. 'Hurry up and get showered and dressed, you two. I'm hungry.'

'If you'll give me half an hour, I'll put supper on,' said Hester breathlessly. So much for avoiding Connah in her swimsuit.

'I'll help,' said Lowri, hurrying up the steps in front of them.

'We'll all help,' said Connah firmly. 'This is Hester's holiday too.'

By the time Lowri and Hester were both dry and dressed and the cases had been unpacked it was rather more than half an hour, and Connah had pre-empted Hester by taking their supper out to the loggia himself.

'It's just cold turkey and spiced ham, and tomatoes and bread and cheese and so on tonight, as I asked,' he said, looking pleased with himself. 'Plus a pudding Flavia made for us.'

'Thank you,' said Hester, taken aback by this reversal of their usual roles.

'My pleasure.'

As they sat down to their meal the sun began to set and Connah lit the shaded lamp on the table. He filled two glasses with sparkling white wine, and one with *limonata,* then raised his glass in a toast. 'Happy holiday, ladies.'

'You too, Daddy,' said Lowri happily.

'Yes, indeed,' agreed Hester. 'Thank you very much for inviting me.'

Lowri stared at her blankly. 'We couldn't have come without you!'

'If we had, Hester,' said Connah wryly, 'I'd be a broken man by the time we got back if I had to cope with Lowri on my own for four weeks.'

'I'm not that bad!' protested his daughter. 'Oh, look. The stars are coming out and there's a little moon at the edge of the sky over there by the pool.'

'All laid on specially for you,' teased her father.

It was a magical evening, not least because Connah Carey Jones was a very different man on holiday. He treated Hester as though they were just two people enjoying the company of the child and each other, with no hint of employer and employee. The impression grew stronger when Connah insisted that he and Lowri would remove dishes and fetch the pudding while Hester just sat there and counted stars.

'I will also make the coffee,' he announced as he came back with a dish of *pannacotta*, the national favourite, for dessert.

'There's a caramel sauce underneath the creamy bit,' Hester told the child. 'Shall I spoon it over yours?'

'Yes, *please*,' said Lowri, licking her lips. 'Are you having some, Daddy?'

He shook his head. 'Not for me. I'll stick with *pecorino* and another hunk of this wonderful bread.'

They lingered at the table while the sky grew dark and the stars grew brighter. The warm air was fragrant with flowers and new-cut grass and some other scent Connah told Hester came from a herb bed under the kitchen window.

'Jay Anderson planted it for his wife, and Flavia is only too delighted to make use of it. The scent is a mixture of rosemary, thyme, sage—and basil, of course, and probably a few other things I've never heard of.' Connah leaned back, relaxed. 'I must tell Jay that if ever he feels like selling the place to think of me first.'

Lowri gazed at him, round-eyed. 'Would you really buy it, Daddy?'

'In the unlikely event that Jay and Stella would want to sell, yes. But they won't part with it, *cariad*. And who could blame them?'

Jay Anderson had installed a large television and DVD player in the sitting room, but for once Lowri made no protest when Connah said it was late and she must go straight to bed so that Hester could come back downstairs and relax for a while in the warm night air.

'You can read another chapter of that book you're devouring,' said Hester.

The child embraced her father with enthusiasm, but a yawn overtook her as she went inside with Hester. 'I quite fancy going to bed in that dear little room next to yours,' she admitted sleepily. 'I was too excited to sleep much last night.'

Within minutes the face-washing and teeth-brushing routine was over and Lowri was tucked under the snow-white covers on the bed. 'I'm too tired to read tonight,' she said, yawning. 'Will you kiss me goodnight, Hester?'

Touched, Hester bent to kiss the smooth, flushed cheek, brushed a hand over the silky dark hair, then said goodnight and went quietly from the room to go downstairs to Connah.

As always, his requirements had been clearly stated. Otherwise, since this was a different situation, in a different country, Hester would have been uncertain what to do once Lowri was in bed. She felt a *frisson* of pure pleasure at spending time alone with Connah in these circumstances, as she took a few minutes in her room to brush her hair and touch a lipstick to her mouth. Her thin cotton dress was an old one, but the gentian-blue shade deepened the colour of her eyes and the wide skirt was more holiday-friendly than the clothes she wore in Albany Square. The face that looked back at her from the mirror was flushed from the sun and the swim and the sheer pleasure of the evening. Four weeks, she told it firmly. After that it would nearly be time to leave Connah and Lowri and go on to pastures new in Yorkshire. Where she would miss Lowri badly when she was looking after a newborn baby. She would miss Lowri's father even more. She took in a deep breath and smiled at her reflection. Instead of anticipating future pain, right now it was time to join Connah—and make the most of present pleasure.

CHAPTER SEVEN

CONNAH was waiting impatiently when Hester joined him on the loggia. 'At last! Did Lowri con you into reading the book to her, instead?'

'No, she was too tired.' She smiled. 'By the time I'd finished tidying her room she was asleep.'

'You were a long time coming down,' he commented, pulling out a chair for her. 'I thought you might have had second thoughts and gone to bed.'

'Not without saying goodnight!'

'Goodnight, Connah,' he ordered. 'We're supposed to be on first name terms, but so far, Hester, I've yet to hear mine from you.'

'I find it difficult,' she said awkwardly.

'Why?'

'For obvious reasons.'

He eyed her challengingly. 'How did you address your last employers?'

'As Leo and Julia,' she admitted, 'but it was a very informal household.'

'So is mine. From now on you say Connah, or I shall address you as Miss Ward.' He smiled suddenly. 'Loosen up, Hester. This is a holiday. Forget your scruples and enjoy the break from humdrum routine in Albany Square.'

Hester couldn't help laughing. 'During my brief but eventful time in Albany Square, life has been anything but humdrum.'

'That's better—you should laugh more often,' he approved. 'Have a glass of wine.'

Oh, why not? thought Hester. 'Thank you,' she said sedately.

After a comfortable silence Connor asked what she would like to do the next day. 'The local shops will be shut on a Sunday, but we could drive somewhere, if you like.'

'Speaking in professional nanny mode,' said Hester, 'I think a day of doing nothing much at all would be good for Lowri after the journey today. She can swim and sunbathe, maybe watch a DVD or even take a nap when the sun gets hot, and if she gets restless I can take her for a walk later when it's cooler. Then, maybe, on Monday you could drive us into Greve and drink coffee in the square while Lowri and I look round the shops.'

'I'll come shopping with you,' said Connah, surprising her. 'And afterwards I'll take you to lunch somewhere.'

'Thank you. Lowri would adore that.' So would Hester. 'By the way, when you need time to yourself with your laptop, just say the word and I'll keep Lowri occupied.'

Connah stretched out in his chair with a sigh of pleasure. 'At the moment the thought of even opening my laptop is too much effort. Maybe I'll just stick to lotus-eating for a while. God knows, this is the ideal place for it.'

'You said you'd stayed here before?'

'Twice. But on both occasions the house was packed with the Anderson family and various friends. Great fun, but definitely not peaceful.' He turned to look at her. 'I'll join you and Lowri to laze the day away tomorrow—including the daily swim.'

Hester liked his programme very much. Even the swim.

'Tell me,' he said idly, as though the answer were of no particular importance, 'why was there such a gap between your last job and the next one, Hester?'

'It wasn't planned. When Leo and Julia won the leads in a new television series in LA, I looked for another post right away and sorted the one in Yorkshire quite quickly. But the Herricks were needed in LA weeks sooner than expected and the Rutherford baby isn't due until early October, so a temporary job seemed the ideal way to fill in the time.'

'Wouldn't you have liked a holiday before getting down to work again?'

Hester was silent for a while. 'I'd been asked to go to the South of France,' she said at last, gazing out at the starlit garden, 'but the holiday fell through at the last minute.'

'So what went wrong?'

'The friend who invited me cancelled at the eleventh hour.'

'Why?'

'He received a sudden job offer and barely had time to apologise before boarding the plane to head west for fame and fortune.'

Connah shot her a searching glance. 'Were you unhappy about that, Hester?'

She shook her head. 'Only where the cancelled holiday was concerned.'

'You mentioned fame and fortune, so I take it the man is an actor. Would I know him?'

She shrugged. 'You might. He played a psychopath in one of those film *noir* type thrillers recently. It won him rave reviews, which led to a role as Julia's wicked brother in the American series she's starring in with Leo. Though the fact that he really is Julia's little brother probably helped with that.'

'What's his name?'

'Keir McBride.'

Connah shook his head. 'Never heard of him.'

Hester chuckled. 'He'd be mortified if he knew.'

'Is he very pretty?'

'Very. He's fair, like Julia, with bright blue eyes and angelic good looks. They made his psychotic performance all the more chilling.'

Connah's face looked stern in the dim light. 'Had you known him long?'

'Off and on for the three years I worked for his sister. But in the period before the Herricks' big break he was out of a job and came to "rest" for a while at their house. Leo and Julia were out in the evenings, performing in their respective shows, so Keir took to spending time with me most evenings after I put the twins to bed. We got on so well he asked if I fancied a holiday with him in the Herricks' farmhouse in the Dordogne once Julia and Leo left for LA. But then, out of the blue, he got the offer of a lifetime, so no holiday.'

'Will you see him again?' said Connor, seized with a sudden desire to rearrange the actor's angelic face.

'I doubt it. If Keir makes a success of his part in the series—which he will because, pretty face or not, he's a brilliant actor—he's bound to get more offers over there. If things go well for him, I doubt that he'll come back to this country any time soon.' Hester smiled crookedly. 'Believe me, it was no romance. Keir was out of work, short of funds and I was right there, captive company for him every evening. The bird in the hand.'

Connah gave her a searching look. 'If you'd gone with the Herricks to LA you could have gone on seeing McBride. Why did you refuse?'

'It was too far away from my family. Also, at that stage Keir was based in the UK and wanted us to see something of each other now and then. But in the end he went off to LA too.' Hester shrugged. 'At which point I answered a couple of advertisements for temporary summer jobs and one of them was yours.'

'Which is my great good fortune—and Lowri's.' He frowned. 'You do so much more than just look after her, I should be paying you a far larger salary than I do.'

'Certainly not,' she said promptly. 'A free holiday in a place like this is recompense enough.'

'I wouldn't call it free exactly,' he said dryly. 'Looking after Lowri is no sinecure.'

'But I enjoy it. If I didn't, I'd be in the wrong job, Connah!'

'At last,' he said in triumph. 'You finally brought yourself to say my name.'

She hadn't brought herself to it at all. His name had tripped off her tongue all too easily. Probably because here in this starlit, scented garden the world they'd left behind could have been on another planet.

'I wonder how Sam's getting on,' she said idly.

'After I rang my mother to tell her we'd arrived I gave Sam a call while you were putting Lowri to bed. All's well in the house and Sam was about to take a stroll down to his local for a pint. I thought he'd have seized the chance of a holiday abroad somewhere, but apparently he had his fill of globe-trotting when he was in the army. He prefers Albany Square in peace and quiet on his own.'

'So he told me.' To her embarrassment, Hester was suddenly overwhelmed by a huge yawn.

Connah smiled. 'You're tired. I'm sorry to lose your company, but I think it's time you went to bed, Hester. You'll have a full day tomorrow—as usual.'

Hester rose at once to assert herself in housekeeper role before she lost sight of why she was really here. 'I'll take these glasses into the kitchen on my way. Goodnight.'

'Goodnight, Connah,' he corrected.

'Goodnight, Connah,' she repeated obediently.

'Much better,' he said, and gave her the smile which knocked her defences flat.

The following day was spent as planned—swimming, reading or just lazing in the sun. Connah joined Hester and Lowri for their morning swim, then retreated to his room afterwards to ring his mother again. She assured him she was feeling better and asked to speak to Lowri. He beckoned from his balcony and the child came running upstairs to chatter happily to her grandmother about the Casa Girasole and the wonderful time she was having with Daddy and Hester.

'Lowri sounds very happy, Connah,' said his mother, when Lowri had raced back down to the garden. 'Miss Ward is obviously doing an excellent job with her.'

'So much so that I'm not looking forward to the day she leaves us.'

'Lowri will be in school soon after that. And next school holiday, God willing, I shall be fit enough to take charge of my granddaughter myself.'

'Of course you will,' he said firmly, and wished he could believe it. 'With that in mind, take good care of yourself, Mother. I'll talk to you again tomorrow.'

Connah returned to his small balcony to look down at the pool. Hester was lying back in a garden chair under an umbrella, listening as Lowri perched at her feet to read aloud from one of the books provided by the school for the summer holiday. He smiled wryly. He wouldn't have thought of bringing the books with them, but Hester had produced one straight after the morning swim. And Lowri had begun reading without the slightest protest. Whatever Hester wanted, Lowri would do, Connah realised. It was a disturbing thought. He rubbed his chin, frowning. Lowri had been fond of Alice, who had been a fixture all her young life and taken for granted. But because Lowri had settled to life away at school so well there'd been no problem when Alice left to get married.

The situation with Hester was very different. Lowri had grown attached to her so quickly she would miss Hester desperately when the time came to part. And so, by God, would he! Thrusting the thought from his mind, Connah put the phone in his pocket and went downstairs to tell Flavia that she could take the following day off; they would bring food home with them from Greve for supper. Flavia thanked him, beaming, explaining that the unexpected holiday gave her the opportunity to visit her niece. Connah then went out to the pool to tell Lowri about the proposed outing.

'Brilliant,' said his daughter, delighted. 'I can buy postcards to send to Grandma, and Moira and Robert, and Chloe and Sam. Gosh, my throat's dry. I've been reading so long I'm thirsty.'

'I'll get you a drink,' said Hester, getting up, but Lowri pushed her back in her chair.

'I can get it myself, and practice my Italian on Flavia at the same time.' She ran off, long legs flying, and Connah took her place beside Hester.

'She's growing up before my eyes. It's frightening. But should she be on first name terms with your parents?'

'It was their idea,' Hester assured him.

'Good. By the way, I told Flavia to take the day off tomorrow.'

'No problem. I can cook.'

'No cooking. We'll buy food for a cold supper while we're in Greve.'

Hester smiled her thanks. 'Is that the kind of thing you did when your mother shared your holiday?'

Connah shook his head. 'Mother's holiday of choice is a fully-catered hotel in Devon or Tenby in Wales. She doesn't like flying. And we rarely stayed more than ten days or so.'

Hester sat up, surprised. 'But Lowri told me she'd been to France last year.'

'That was a school trip. My mother thought she was far too young to go, but I find it hard to refuse Lowri anything. So far her demands have been easy to meet.' His face darkened. 'As she gets older, things will change.'

'Don't worry too much. I think Lowri knows exactly where to draw the line.'

He smiled crookedly. 'I discovered that for myself last week when you were out. She played me like a fish at bedtime until I blew the whistle.'

Lowri came racing back to tell them Flavia said lunch would be ready in ten minutes.

'How did you understand what she said?' asked Connah, amused.

'I'm picking up a word or two, so lunch will be at *mezzogiorno*,' she said with a flourish. 'That's midday, and it's in ten minutes. Eight now,' she added, looking at her watch. 'It's spaghetti with yummy red sauce—Flavia let me taste it. And for supper tonight it's *pollo cacciatore*. That's some kind of chicken. It just has to be heated up when we need it, and it's all in one pot and smells gorgeous.'

Her father chuckled. 'One way to get fluent in a foreign language!'

Hester got up. 'Right then, Lowri. Just time for a wash and tidy-up before lunch.'

'You sound just like Alice sometimes,' remarked Lowri as they walked up the garden.

Something to watch, thought Hester, biting her lip.

'You're not a bit like her in other ways, though,' added Lowri. 'Alice is pretty, but she's not slim like you. She's very smiley and cuddly, though.'

'And I'm not?'

Lowri eyed Hester objectively as they went upstairs. 'When you smile it sort of lights up your face, and I notice it more because you don't smile all the time. And you use make-up and scent, you have a great haircut, and your clothes are sort of plain but always look just right, like Chloe's mother. And you're young,' she added as the final accolade. 'Mrs Powell said Alice was very lucky to catch a husband at her age.'

Poor old Alice, thought Hester. 'And what age would that be?'

'I'm not sure. More than thirty, anyway.' Lowri looked at her curiously as they went into the bathroom. 'How old are you, Hester?'

'Twenty-seven—and I'm hungry, so let's hurry it up.'

After Flavia's excellent lunch, all three were a little somnolent as they sat at the table on the loggia.

'Lord knows I don't feel like it, but I must do some work this afternoon,' announced Connah, yawning.

'I feel sleepy too,' said Lowri, surprised.

'Then why not have a nap on your bed and leave Hester in peace for a couple of hours?'

'Later we'll have a swim,' promised Hester.

'OK,' said Lowri, getting up. 'I'll read for a while. You don't have to come up with me,' she added, but Hester was already on her feet.

'I want my book. I fancy a nice peaceful read by the pool.'

'Make sure you keep under an umbrella,' advised Connah.

'Alice can't sit in the sun, she gets all red and shiny,' said Lowri as they went upstairs. 'But you don't, Hester.'

'Genetics—olive skin like my father. Right, then. When you've had a rest, get into your bikini and join me by the pool.'

'Have you got a bikini?' asked Lowri as she began to undress.

'Yes.'

'Wear it this afternoon!'

'I'll see.'

'Oh, please, Hester. I bet you look really cool in it.'

'I'll think about it. Enjoy your book, and I'll see you later.'

In her own room Hester exchanged her shorts and T-shirt for a sea-green bikini bought for France. She eyed herself in the mirror and thought why not? She added the long filmy shirt bought to go with it, collected her book, hat and sunglasses and the tote bag that held everything else and went downstairs to compliment Flavia on their lunch. The afternoon sun was hot as she made for the pool and she was grateful for the shade of an umbrella as she settled down with the book she'd started in bed the night before. The bed had been supremely comfortable and the room cool and airy, but sleep had been elusive. The sounds of the night through the open windows had made her restless because, added to the mix, she knew Connah was sitting alone on the loggia.

Hester was absorbed in the novel when a shadow fell across her book and she looked up with a smile, expecting Connah. But a complete stranger stood smiling back at her. A handsome Italian stranger at that.

She shot upright, pulling her shirt together.

'*Perdoneme*, I startled you,' he said apologetically. 'I thought you were the Signora Anderson. Permit me to introduce myself. I am Pierluigi Martinelli.'

'Hester Ward,' she said formally. 'How do you do?'

'*Piacere*. You are here on holiday?'

'Yes.' Hester cast a look back at the house, relieved to see Connah about to join them, hand outstretched to the visitor.

'Hello, Luigi. I didn't know you were here.'

'Connah, *come estai*!' The two men shook hands. 'I have just arrived. I came through the woods and along the private path into your garden. I am at the *Castello* for a while.'

'Have you met Hester?'

'We introduced ourselves, yes,' said Luigi, smiling at her. 'Are the Andersons here?'

'No. Just Hester, myself and my daughter.' Connah took Hester's hand. 'Darling, would you be an angel and ask Flavia to bring us some coffee?'

Darling? Hester gathered up her belongings. 'I'll get Lowri up while I'm there.'

Grateful for the long, filmy shirt which veiled most of her from the Italian's appreciative gaze, Hester went quickly up the garden and into the house to announce, as best she could, that they had a visitor.

'*Caffè, per favore, Flavia, per* signore Martinelli.'

The name had a dramatic effect on the plump little woman. '*Il Conte? Maddonnina mia—subito, subito!*' Flavia went into overdrive as she began laying a silver tray with the Andersons' best china.

Amused, Hester went upstairs to find Lowri already changed for her swim. 'Your father has a visitor, so put a shirt on top. I won't be a moment. I'm going to change.'

The glowing face fell. 'But you said you were going to swim with me!'

'And I will, later, but right now I'm going to get dressed.'

Lowri gave an admiring look at the sea-green bikini. 'Do you have to?'

'Yes, I do. Go on down and meet the visitor, if you like. I'll be five minutes.'

'I'll wait for you,' offered Lowri.

'Flavia's making coffee for the visitor. Why not run down and ask if you can carry something to the pool for her?'

'OK. But don't be long.'

Hester pulled on a white cotton jersey shift at top speed, the word 'darling' reverberating in her head. At last, her hair caught up in a careless knot, gold thong sandals on her feet, dark glasses in place, she went downstairs to the kitchen where, with many apologies and much hand-waving, Flavia explained that the cakes meant for dessert after supper had been served to *Il Conte* with his coffee.

'*Non importa,*' said Hester airily, and took the ice-filled jug of lemonade Flavia handed to her.

As she strolled down the descending tiers of flower beds towards the pool, Hester watched the two men standing together, with Lowri between them like a small referee. They were both dark, mature men, but Signor Martinelli, or *Il Conte* as Flavia called him, was unmistakably Latin. He wore elegant casual clothes, as expensively cut as his glossy black hair, and had an air of swagger about him even in repose. Connah's darkness of hair and eye were, at least to Hester's eye, unmistakably Celt. He was the taller of the two, with a hint of toughness and power about his broad-shouldered physique which appealed to Hester far more than the grace of the urbane Italian.

'Ah, Hester,' Connah said, smiling, as he took the jug from her. 'Perhaps you'll pour for us while Lowri hands round the cakes?'

'Certainly.' She looked enquiringly at Luigi Martinelli, who promptly took the seat beside her as she sat down. 'You like your coffee black?'

'*Grazie.*' He eyed her with open appreciation. 'And how do you like my homeland, Miss Hester? You have travelled here before?'

'Not here exactly. I've been to Venice, but this is my first time in Tuscany, which is so beautiful, how could I not like it? Please, have one of Flavia's cakes.'

He took one from the plate Lowri was offering, smiling fondly at the child. 'And how old are you, *carina*?'

'Ten,' she said quietly, shy in the presence of this exotic visitor.

'You are a tall lady for ten,' he said with admiration.

'Is Sophia with you?' asked Connah.

'No. My wife is in Rome. Where else? She does not care for the *campagna*.' Luigi shrugged. 'But from time to time I experience *la nostalgia* for the tranquillity of my old home. When I heard that Casa Girasole was occupied I assumed that the Andersons were here and came to invite them to dinner tonight. But I would count it a great privilege, Connah, if you and your ladies would honour me with your company instead.'

Connah shook his head decisively. 'Sorry, Luigi. We keep early hours here to suit my daughter. Another time, perhaps.'

'Of course.' Luigi drained his cup and stood up. 'It was a great pleasure to meet you, Miss Hester, also you, Miss Lowri. A charming name,' he added. 'I have never heard it before.'

'It's Welsh for Laura,' she volunteered shyly.

He startled the child by bowing gracefully over her hand before bidding the others goodbye. 'I hope to see you again soon. Ciao.'

Luigi Martinelli strolled off the way he'd come, knowing—and probably enjoying the fact—that three pairs of eyes watched him go.

'What a nice man,' said Lowri, taking the chair next to Hester. 'Can I have some *limonata*, please?'

Connah raised an eyebrow at Hester as she poured it. 'What did you think of our local sprig of nobility? I should have introduced him as Count Pierluigi Martinelli. The local *Castello* has been in his family for centuries.'

'Flavia mentioned the title as she rushed to make coffee for him.' Hester smiled. 'You note that the Andersons' best china was produced for *Il Conte*.'

'Flavia has lived here all her life. In her mind, she numbers God, the local priest and Luigi as most important in the local pecking order—though not necessarily in that order. As a girl she was a maid up at the *Castello*, and Nico, her husband, is Luigi's gardener.'

'Is it a real castle with turrets and things?' asked Lowri, fascinated. 'I would have liked to see it, Daddy.'

He smiled ruefully. 'Sorry, *cariad*, I should have consulted you before turning Luigi down.'

'We couldn't have gone tonight anyway,' she reminded him. 'We've got Flavia's special chicken dinner.'

'So we have.' Connah picked up the tray. 'I'll leave the lemonade, but I'll take the rest in for Flavia, then I think I'll change and have a swim.'

'Me too,' said Lowri promptly, stripping off her shirt. 'Are you going to change back into your bikini, Hester?'

'I don't think so. You can have your swim with your father,' said Hester, avoiding Connah's eye.

'Spoilsport,' he murmured as his daughter jumped into the pool.

Hester was happy to sit where she was, watching as father and daughter played in the pool. Connah's muscular body was broad in the shoulder and slim-hipped, also deeply tanned, probably, thought Hester, by some other foreign sun, in striking contrast to his daughter, whose fair skin was already acquiring a glow, courtesy of the Tuscan sun, but it was a different tone from her father's. Lowri's eyes and skin obviously came from her mother and, as she often did, Hester wondered about the woman Connah had cared for so deeply. After the one startling incident when he'd showed his emotions on the subject, he hadn't mentioned her again. And why should he? Theirs was a professional, working relationship, she reminded herself. On Connah's side, anyway.

Eventually, after much splashing and laughter, father and daughter went in the house to shower and dress. When Connah announced that he was going to do some work before dinner Lowri asked him if she could walk to the village with Hester.

'Flavia says they have good *gelato* in the shop there,' she said eagerly.

'How you do love your ice cream,' he mocked. 'But I'd rather you didn't go without me, and I can't come right now. We'll all walk there another time.'

Lowri pouted a little, but brightened when Hester suggested that instead they ask Flavia for instructions about heating her *pollo cacciatore*. 'We'll ask her to teach us the Italian words for things in the kitchen.'

This programme met with warm approval and a lively hour was spent in the kitchen with a delighted Flavia, who enjoyed the impromptu Italian lesson as much as her students. Afterwards she said her farewells, wished them a happy time in Greve the next day and set off down the road on her bicycle with all the panache of a competitor in the Tour de France.

'She's so jolly and nice,' said Lowri, and gave Hester an impish grin. 'A lot different from Grandma's Mrs Powell.'

Since Flavia had already laid the table on the loggia and the pot of chicken merely needed heating when they were ready to eat, Hester suggested it might be a good idea to sit quietly in the *salone* with a book until it was time for supper.

'Will you sit with me?' said Lowri quickly.

'Of course.' But as they settled down together Hester felt troubled. Lowri was becoming far too dependent on her. Which was delightful in one way, because Hester was very fond of the child. But when the day came to say goodbye, as it always did, the parting would be even more painful than in the past. The other children she'd cared for had cried bitterly when she'd left, but unlike Lowri they'd had their mothers to comfort them. Although Lowri had Connah and her grandmother, Hester consoled herself. Children were resilient. She would soon recover once she was back in school with Chloe and all her friends.

The supper was a great success. On instruction from Flavia, Hester served a first course of Parma ham with ripe figs bursting with juice. The savoury *cacciatore* that followed tasted as delicious as its aroma, but it was so substantial that when Hester offered the depleted selection of cakes for dessert not even Lowri had room for one.

'Gosh, I'm full,' she said, yawning.

'In that case, to let your supper go down you'd better stroll round the garden for a while with Daddy while I clear away,' said Hester, collecting plates. 'You can watch the moon rise over the pool.'

'I'll make coffee when you come down after Lowri's in bed, Hester,' said Connah. 'Come on then, *cariad*,' he said, holding out his hand to his daughter. 'Quick march.'

Later, when the kitchen was tidy and Lowri seen safely to bed, Hester went down to join Connah. The scent of freshly made coffee mingled deliciously with the garden scents of the night and she resumed her chair with a sigh of pleasure.

'How beautiful it is here.'

'But it gets cold in the winter when the *tramontana* blows,' said Connah, pouring coffee. 'I was here once with the Andersons for New Year's Eve. By the way, that was a very meaningful look you gave me regarding the stroll in the garden with Lowri.'

'Yes.' Hester braced herself. 'Forgive me if I'm overstepping the mark, but I think you should spend more time with her on your own. Not,' she added hastily, 'because I want time off or because I don't enjoy her company. I do. So much that Lowri won't be the only one to feel sad when we say goodbye. But instead of always having me around I think, or at least I'm suggesting, that you should take her out now and again on your own, just the two of you. Maybe take her to visit the *Castello*, or walk with her into the village.'

'Is that why you seemed abstracted over our wonderful dinner?'

'Yes. She wouldn't sit and read earlier unless I did too.' Hester raised worried eyes to his. 'If she's with me all the time, it will be even more painful when I leave. As I know from bitter experience. The Herrick twins sobbed so much when I left it tore me in pieces. Julia had chickened out of telling them I wasn't going with them to America, so when they found out at the very last minute it was rough on all of us.'

Connah sat in silence for a while, sipping his coffee. 'If,' he said at last, 'you find this part of your job so painful, isn't it time you found some other way to earn a living?'

'I've been thinking of it quite a lot lately, but though I'm top of the tree at what I do, I'm not qualified for anything else. Besides,' she added with a sigh, 'it was always a vocation for me rather than just a way of earning my living.'

'So that's the reason for your sober mood tonight? I thought it was something quite different,' said Connah casually. 'Like being addressed as "darling" this afternoon, maybe.'

CHAPTER EIGHT

THE silence which followed this statement grew too long for comfort. Hester drained her coffee cup and set it down, then refilled it. 'More for you?' she asked politely.

'Thank you. So tell me. Were you annoyed?' Connah said bluntly.

'Surprised, not annoyed.' She shrugged as she poured his coffee. 'You don't strike me as someone who bandies meaningless endearments about, so I assumed you had a practical reason.'

'You assumed right.' Connah leaned back in his chair, watching her, his long legs crossed at the ankles. 'I didn't like the way Luigi Martinelli was looking at you.'

Hester stared at him blankly. 'How *was* he looking at me?'

'You were wearing a few bits of green silk and a transparent shirt. How do you think he was looking at you? He's a man, for God's sake, and Italian at that.'

Hester was glad the covering darkness hid the rush of indignant colour in her face. 'I would remind you that I was not expecting a stranger to appear in the garden when Lowri coaxed me to wear the bikini.' Her chin lifted. 'Don't worry, it won't happen again!'

'Pity. That green colour looks spectacular against your tan. No wonder Luigi couldn't take his eyes off you. But you won't have any trouble from him,' Connah added with satisfaction. 'He knows the rules.'

'Which are?' she demanded.

'No mention was made of your official role in the household so now, naturally, he thinks the role is more personal—'

'Than the one I'm paid for,' she said stonily.

'Are you saying you'd have welcomed Luigi's attentions?'

She glared at him. 'Certainly not. He's a total stranger, also married. You mentioned his wife, remember.'

'Mainly because he'd rather forget he has one,' said Connah, shrugging. 'Luigi possesses a meaningless title but a very old name and impeccable lineage. Sophia inherited a pile of money from her wheeler-dealer Papa. She wanted Luigi's aristocratic pedigree and he needed her cash, which just about sums up the relationship, according to Jay Anderson. Since the birth of their son, they lead separate lives.'

'How sad.'

He shot her a look. 'You, I assume, would only marry for love.'

Hester was silenced for a moment. 'The subject has never really come up,' she said at last, 'but if it did, respect and rapport would be my priorities. Loving someone to desperation is not for me.'

'But you were willing to spend a holiday in the South of France with the actor.'

Hester nodded serenely. 'The offer was too tempting to turn down.'

'Then I gave you the chance of one in Tuscany instead. And there was no backing out of this one at the last minute,' he added.

'But that's different,' she protested.

'Why?'

'It's my job. I'm very grateful you asked me to come here with you and Lowri, of course, but you're paying me to work for you wherever we are.'

'A very cold-blooded way to look at it,' he said morosely and shot her a look she didn't care for. 'If the trip to France had come off, would you have shared bed as well as board with your Romeo?'

Hester stood up and put the cups on the coffee tray. 'The fact that I work for you, Mr Carey Jones, doesn't give you the right to ask personal questions.'

'I disagree. The moral welfare of my daughter gives me every right,' he retorted, getting to his feet.

'I was not looking after your daughter at the time,' she reminded him, dangerously quiet. 'Not counting breaks at home, the only holiday I've had in years was a package trip to Spain with school friends in my teens. Once I started work, I went straight from my first job to the Herricks. And looking after babies means constant responsibility, long, irregular hours and a lot of broken sleep. So yes. I was human enough to accept the offer of a free holiday in the sun before starting work in Yorkshire.'

'A long speech, but you still haven't answered my question, Hester.'

She gave him a haughty look. 'I don't intend to. Goodnight.' She picked up the tray and took it into the kitchen to wash up and with supreme effort did so quietly, instead of bashing dishes about in a rage.

'I apologise, Hester,' said Connah, coming up behind her so quietly that she almost dropped the cup she was drying.

'You startled me,' she said tightly.

'Come out again and have a glass of wine. It's too early to go to bed.'

'No, thank you.'

Connah looked down at her, his hard eyes wry. 'I've obviously offended you past all forgiveness.'

'I work for you,' she said shortly. 'I can't afford to be offended.'

'Dammit, Hester, that's hitting below the belt! I know damn well I have no right to probe into your private life.' He took the cup from her and put it on the tray, then fetched a bottle of wine from the refrigerator and gave her a smile she tried hard to resist. 'It's a pity to go to bed so early on a night like this. Can you honestly say you'll sleep if you do?'

'I'll read.'

'You can do that later. Come out and talk for a while.'

Because Hester had no real desire to go to bed, she swallowed her pride, went back outside and even accepted the glass of wine Connah poured for her.

'So what do you want in Greve tomorrow?' he asked.

'Postcards, some food for supper. Real local fare from small grocery shops rather than a supermarket,' she added.

'Whatever you want, as long as it doesn't involve cooking. I meant what I said. This must be a holiday for you before you go on to your next job. Particularly in the light of our recent discussion,' he added dryly. 'Will you enjoy looking after a newborn baby?'

Hester shrugged, resigned. 'I've done it before in my last post, twins at that. But, much as I love babies, it's a lot easier to look after someone like Lowri. And not just because she dresses and feeds herself,' she added with a chuckle. 'She's such fun and good company. And she sleeps all night!'

Connah laughed. 'Ah, yes, the broken nights. That's one part you can't be looking forward to.'

'I won't be doing it alone. Sarah Rutherford intends to feed the baby herself if she can, but I'll be on hand to see to the rest. At least there's just one to look after this time.'

'I don't know how you do it,' he said, grimacing. 'I wasn't around much when Lowri was at that stage. My mother and Alice bore the brunt of it.'

Because he'd had to cope with his wife's death, thought Hester with compassion, then eyed him quizzically when he gave a sudden chuckle.

'Talking of Alice, I wonder how Mal and Owen will cope when the baby arrives.'

'With someone of Alice's experience, perfectly well, I imagine. By the way, Lowri told me that Alice isn't at all like me.'

He let out a bark of laughter. 'God, no. Nice, sweet creature though she is, I wouldn't be sitting here with her like this.'

'Why not?'

'She's very nervous around me, for a start. In the unlikely event that I asked her to sit and chat over a glass of wine, she'd run a mile.' He shot a look at Hester. 'Alice is a sweet, ordinary young woman from the village near Bryn Derwen and I'll always be grateful to her because she came to us at a time when we needed her so desperately. I will never forget that. But she's very different from you, Hester.'

'In what way?'

'You're good looking, well read, and your qualifications are impeccable. Alice has no professional qualifications, other than willingness to work and her unbounded love of children.'

'Then I salute her, because Lowri is a credit to her—and to your mother, of course,' said Hester, and looked across at Connah. 'And last, but very definitely not least, to you—the most important person in her life.'

'I know,' he said soberly. 'And it's a huge responsibility.' He got up to refill her glass, but she shook her head.

'No more, thanks.'

Connah sat down again, looking out over the starlit garden. 'A pity we can't do this by the pool.'

'It's too far away from the house—and Lowri.'

'Exactly. I've been thinking about you a lot lately,' he added, startling her. 'I've tried hard to remember you as you were when I first saw you all those years ago. But all I can bring to mind is a teenager with long blonde curls and huge eyes.'

'The curls were courtesy of a perm and the eyes looked huge

because I was into heavy-duty eye make-up at the time.' She laughed. 'I was also rather chubby, but you've been kind enough to gloss over that.'

'From the fleeting glimpse I had of you by the pool this afternoon, it's not a word that applies any more.' He raised an eyebrow. 'As a matter of interest, would you have stayed in the bikini if I'd been there alone with you and Lowri?'

'Yes,' she said honestly. 'Lowri pleaded so I wore it.'

'Then wear it again, when we're safe from intruders.'

'I don't think so.'

'You mean it's not approved nanny wear?'

She nodded. 'Or housekeeper wear.'

He chuckled. 'A bit different from the archetypal Mrs Danvers.'

'So you've read Rebecca too.'

'Afraid not—I saw the film. It's one of the few films I've ever seen. I'm not a movie buff.'

Hester eyed him in surprise. 'You must have watched one of Lowri's DVDs with her?'

'No. I keep to chess,' Connah admitted.

'A suitable film is another good way to keep her company while she spends a quiet hour out of the sun. Try watching one with her some time. She'd love it.'

'Yes, Nanny.'

Hester chuckled. 'Sorry.'

Connah shook his head. 'Don't be. I'll take all the advice I can get. Pity the single male parent of a girl child.'

'Speaking professionally, I think you make an excellent job of it.'

'Thank you. But it's going to get harder as she gets older.' He sighed deeply. 'And my mother's convalescence is much slower than I'd hoped. It's going to be some time before she's in any kind of shape to look after an energetic child like Lowri.' He shot a look at her. 'I know the original agreement was six weeks, but if you're not due in Yorkshire until October, Hester, would you consider staying on with us for an extra week or two to get Lowri ready to go back to school?'

'Yes, of course,' she said without hesitation. 'If it helps you out, I'll be happy to.' More happy than he knew.

Connah smiled at her in relief. 'Thank you, Hester. That should take us up to the middle of September when Lowri starts back. Can you do that?'

'Yes. The Rutherford baby isn't due until mid-October. I promised to start there two weeks beforehand, to help Mrs Rutherford get ready for the big day, so it works in quite well and still gives me time to spend with my mother and Robert first.'

'That's a great load off my mind,' he said, smiling at her. 'But that's a long way off, so until then let's enjoy our summer in sunny Italy. I've never indulged in so much leisure time, so I might as well make the most of it.'

'Everyone needs to unwind now and then.' Hester got up. 'Time I went to bed.'

Connah rose immediately and put a hand on hers. 'Hester, forgive me for my transgression earlier.'

'Of course,' she said lightly, and smiled at him. 'Goodnight.'

The trip to Greve was a huge success. The sun-drenched piazza had originally been square, Connah informed them, but over time buildings with porticos and loggias had encroached on it until now it was a triangle pointing to the church of Santa Croce.

'The church has paintings of the school of Fra Angelico,' he added, then grinned as his daughter made a face. 'All right, don't panic. We'll just look round the shops and buy some postcards since it's your first day in town. Then we'll have some lunch and when Greve wakes up again afterwards we'll buy food for supper.'

For Hester it was hard to remember that this was part of a job she was being paid for as she strolled through the sunlit town with

Connah and Lowri. Never in her wildest dreams of the mysterious Mr Jones when she was young had she imagined a scenario like the one being played out right now. She could almost believe...

'Penny for them,' murmured Connah as Lowri went through every postcard on display before making her choice.

'They're worth far more than that!' Hester assured him.

Lunch was eaten in a restaurant with stone arches and terracotta floors, and best of all to Lowri, a vine-covered pergola with a panoramic view of the sunlit countryside of Chianti.

'Can we eat outside, Daddy?' she asked eagerly.

'Of course, *cariad*.' He turned to Hester. 'Unless you're too hot and would prefer to eat indoors?'

'No, indeed. I'll take all the sun and fresh air I can get.'

Connah had eaten at the restaurant before and, on his recommendation, they all chose light-as-air gnocchi with a sage and butter sauce as a first course, followed by pork roasted with rosemary and served with porcini mushrooms.

'They're just like little pillows,' said Lowri in delight as she tasted the gnocchi.Hester smiled at her lovingly, then flushed when she saw Connah watching her and applied herself to her own meal.

Full of good food, they lingered afterwards in the pergola, the waiters only too pleased to supply them with as much mineral water and coffee as they wanted.

'They take food very seriously here,' said Hester lazily, 'yet they seem quite happy for us to linger as long as we like. There's no rushing to clear away so that someone else can take our place.'

'Not their style at all. Besides, they have enough tables to make that unnecessary,' said Connah, and took his drowsy daughter on his lap. 'Sit quietly for a while, *cariad*, before we make for the shops again. They won't be open for a while, anyway.'

Lowri yawned widely. 'OK.' She snuggled her head into his shoulder and her father smoothed the length of silky hair with a stroking hand as she dozed off.

'I rang my mother last night,' said Hester quietly after a peaceful interval. 'She sent her regards.'

'Return the compliment when you speak to her again.' Connah looked at her across the shining dark head on his shoulder. 'Did your mother ever talk about my companion?'

'Only to say that she was ill. Mother was only too happy for you to stay until the lady was well enough to leave.'

'To my immense gratitude.' His eyes turned towards the sunlit view of vine-covered hillsides. 'I went back to your house a few years later to see your mother, but she was no longer there, of course. And the new owners very rightly felt they weren't at liberty to give me her address.'

'Is that why you came to fetch me the other night? To meet Mother again?'

'Partly.' The dark, intent eyes turned back to hers as though he was about to explain further, but Lowri stirred and sat up, yawning.

'I'm just like a baby, having naps all the time,' she complained.

'This one was very short,' her father said, kissing her nose. 'You go off with Hester to wash your face, then we'll wander round the town again—maybe we'll even force you to explore the church if the shops aren't open yet.'

Lowri slid off his lap at once as Hester got up. 'Do you like churches, Hester?' she asked, sighing.

'I'd like to look round this one. Then we can both write about it on our postcards.'

After a leisurely stroll back to the Santa Croce to admire its neo-classical façade, they went inside to look at the paintings. But Lowri grew restive in the dark interior and they soon went outside again into the sunlight, discussing what food to buy in one of the *alimentares*, the various grocery stores beginning to reopen after their long lunch break.

'We'll definitely get your local fare in one of these, Hester,' said Connah. 'We might as well stock up while we're here.'

Lowri was consulted on every purchase as they bought a great bag of tomatoes, another of peaches, crusty Tuscan bread, ricotta cheese and glossy green spinach.

'Though I'll leave Flavia to deal with the last two,' said Hester, smiling. 'Perhaps she'll make ravioli for us tomorrow.'

'I'll ask her,' said Lowri promptly. 'She likes me.'

'Does she really?' teased Connah. 'Now it's my turn to choose. I want some of those fennel flavoured sausages, and salami, and thin slices of roast turkey breast and ham, and more pecorino cheese. What about you, Hester?'

'Mozzarella and fresh basil, anchovies and olives, and some of those gorgeous baby lettuces, please.'

'Anything else? Speak now while I'm in a good mood, and willing to carry all this stuff to the car.'

'I'll help,' said Lowri promptly.

'I was only teasing, *cariad*. I'm happy to carry anything Hester wants.' Connah grinned. 'After all, she's going to make supper for us tonight.'

It was the kind of day, thought Hester, as they drove back to the Casa Girasole, that she would keep in her mind like a snapshot to look back at and sigh over during a cold Yorkshire winter. But the day wasn't over yet, she consoled herself, and once they were back at the house she sent Lowri off to have a swim with her father while she put the food away.

'If we all help with that, you can swim too,' said Connah, but Hester shook her head.

'That's my job. Besides, I have more idea where everything goes. Then I'll have a shower and start getting supper ready.'

'Can I help?' said Lowri eagerly.

'Of course,' said Hester.

'No cooking,' Connah reminded her.

'My choices were made with that in mind!'

Lowri's swim with her father was surprisingly brief.

'It wasn't the same for her without you,' said Connah as his daughter ran upstairs to shower. He rubbed at his hair with the sleeve of his towelling robe, his smile wry. 'I begin to see what you mean. Tomorrow morning I'll walk into the village with her while you do anything you want.'

'Laundry,' said Hester promptly.

He laughed. 'I was thinking more of a book by the pool with a long drink.'

'I can do that later, when you come back.'

Connah looked back at her as he made for the stairs. 'Did you enjoy the day, Hester?'

'Enormously.' She smiled cheerfully. 'Once Lowri comes down I'll get supper ready. Though after lunch I couldn't imagine wanting to eat another thing today.'

'Well, I can, easily, so be generous.' He paused. 'Not that I need to say that, Hester. Generosity comes naturally to you.' His dark eyes held hers. 'It was a lucky day for me when you came back into my life.'

Hester flushed, deprived of speech for a moment. He held the look a moment longer, then smiled and carried on up the stairs. Hester pulled herself together and went up to check on Lowri's progress and found her wrapped in her robe, gazing out of her window at the view. She turned with a sigh.

'I wish Mr Anderson would sell this house to Daddy. I just love it here. I'm sure Grandma would love it too.' She frowned. 'But she doesn't like flying—perhaps Daddy could bring her here by train if we have another holiday here.'

'In the meantime,' said Hester practically, 'let's get that hair dry so you can dress and help me put supper on.'

One of the many attractions about the holiday for Hester was the lack of hurry about everything. There was no rush to make supper and if Lowri went to bed later than usual it didn't matter in the slightest, because next morning she could sleep until she woke naturally.

'I thought we'd have *bruschetta* first,' said Hester, when a very clean and shining Lowri reported for duty. 'That's thick slices of the bread we bought, with a sprinkling of olive oil and some of those gorgeous tomatoes chopped and topped with basil, anchovies and olives.'

'I've never had anchovies,' said Lowri, inspecting them. 'They're all furry. How can you have furry fish?'

'Magic. But you can have yours without, if you like.'

'Does Daddy like them?'

'I don't know. So we'll just go as far as the tomatoes and basil, and put the olives and anchovies in little pots to add as required.'

'I'll do that, then,' said Lowri promptly. 'What else are we having?'

'Turkey, ham and salami. I'll whip some lemon juice and this wonderful olive oil together for a dressing for the lettuces, and you can get the cheese out.'

Connah crossed the hall later and paused in the kitchen doorway, unnoticed for a moment as he watched Hester and Lowri working together, the gleaming fair head bent to the shiny dark one. Then Hester looked up and smiled and the idea that had germinated in Albany Square, and had been growing in strength ever since, crystallized into certainty.

'It's a hive of activity in here,' he commented, smiling, and Lowri whirled round to beam at him.

'Supper's almost ready, Daddy.'

CHAPTER NINE

AFTER their trip to Greve, all three of them were content to stay at the house the next day. After a leisurely breakfast Connah went indoors to contact John Austin, but Lowri was perfectly happy to take her morning swim with only Hester for company. They played a splashing, noisy game with a ball, with rules that Lowri made up with screams of laughter as she went along until Hester called time at last. While they were towelling themselves dry on the edge of the pool, Lowri stiffened and nudged Hester.

'Look!'

A boy stood watching them from the area where the woods of Martinelli territory edged the grounds of Casa Girasole.

Hester pulled her towelling robe on quickly, wondering if she should call Connah, then heard someone in the distance shouting 'Andrea!' and Luigi Martinelli came racing through the trees with a younger man close behind. He clasped the boy in passionate relief but the boy pushed him away, embarrassed, and spoke urgently to him. Luigi spun round, saw they were being watched, then dismissed the young man with him and brought the boy towards the pool.

'I am intruder again,' he apologised breathlessly as he drew near. '*Buon giorno*, Miss Hester, Miss Lowri, allow me to present my son, Andrea, who has been missing long enough to cause much anxiety. He heard sounds of laughter from your pool and came to investigate.'

'*Piacere*,' said the boy, with a bow that won him a stare from Lowri.

'Hello, Andrea,' said Hester, smiling. 'You like swimming?'

'Very much, *signora*, but we have no pool at the *Castello*,' he said in English more heavily accented than his father's. He turned to an unusually silent Lowri. 'You like to swim?'

She nodded briefly and looked up uncertainly at Hester, who smiled at her reassuringly.

'Why not run and tell Daddy that the Count is here with his son?'

'OK.' Lowri took another look at the boy, then went running up the garden to the house.

'We have interrupted your swim,' apologised Luigi, watching with a wry smile as Connah emerged from the house and strode towards them. '*Buon giorno*. I regret that you have not one but two trespassers today.'

'Good morning.' Connah put his arm round Hester as he smiled at the boy making every nerve in her body tingle in response. 'Hello, there. I'm Connah Carey Jones.'

The slim, dark boy bowed again. 'Andrea Martinelli. Where is the girl, *signore*?'

'My daughter's getting dressed.' Connah smiled down into Hester's face. 'Would you like to do the same, darling? Ask Flavia to bring some coffee to the loggia.'

'Of course.' Hester excused herself and went up the garden into the house, to find that Flavia was already in a fever of activity to provide *Il Conte* and his son with refreshments.

'*Poverino*,' she said as she laid the tray.

With no hope of understanding the answer if she asked why Flavia pitied the boy, Hester went upstairs to change and found Lowri at her window, pulling on shorts and T-shirt as she cast a wary eye at the visitors.

'Are they staying?' she demanded.

'Only for coffee. I'll just throw some clothes on, then we'll go down and show off our exceedingly good manners.' Hester grinned and, after a moment, Lowri grinned back reluctantly.

'OK! I'll wait for you.'

Hester tied up her damp hair with a ribbon and pulled on white linen trousers and blue shirt, hoping that next time she met the Count, if there was a next time, she would be fully dressed from the start. 'Ready?' she asked as she looked into Lowri's room.

'I suppose so. Why has that boy got a girl's name?'

'It's not a girl's name here. It's Italian for Andrew.'

'I hope he doesn't stay long.'

'I thought he looked lonely, standing there by himself. Perhaps he just wants some company.'

Lowri heaved a sigh and followed Hester downstairs. 'He's got a funny accent,' she commented.

The atmosphere on the loggia was much more cordial than on the previous occasion, Hester noted as she sat down to pour coffee.

'Luigi says that young Andrea heard you playing in the pool and couldn't resist coming to have a look,' said Connah, pulling his chair close to Hester's.

'Will you have coffee or lemonade, Andrea?' she asked.

'Lemonade, if you please, *signora*,' he said formally, and Hester filled a glass for Lowri to pass to him. '*Grazie*,' he said, smiling at her.

'So how are you enjoying your holiday, Hester?' asked Luigi.

'Very much. We went to Greve yesterday. It's a delightful town.'

'A pity you are not here in September for the wine fair, which is Chianti's largest,' he commented, accepting a cup of coffee. 'Connah came last year with the Andersons.'

'That was one of the visits I mentioned, Hester,' said Connah. 'Lowri, why not take Andrea for a walk round the garden?'

His daughter shot a bright, accusing look at him, but after another at Hester she got up reluctantly and went off with the boy.

'They are like two little animals, prowling round each other ready to bite,' said Luigi, smiling after them indulgently. His eyes darkened. 'My son gave me a very bad fright earlier when he could not be found.'

Connah nodded. 'I can appreciate that. Don't you have someone to keep watch over him?'

'Of course, his *precettore*, his tutor. But the poor fellow went into the house to answer a call of nature—*scusi*, Hester— and when he came back Andrea had vanished. He ran off in anger because I had just told him I must return to Rome for a day or two tomorrow on business and wish him to stay here while I am away.'

'Is there no one for him to play with at the *Castello*?' asked Hester.

'Apart from the servants, there is only Guido. But I will be away only a short time. It is better he stays here than endure the journey to Rome and back.'

Connah nodded absently, watching the boy dabbling his hands in the pool while Lowri looked on, telling him something he was listening to intently. 'They seem to be getting on well enough now.'

Hester could see that. Andrea appeared to be nodding in enthusiastic agreement to something Lowri was saying, then the boy brushed the water from his hands and the pair ran up the garden together.

'Daddy,' said Lowri, 'can Andrea have lunch here? I told him Flavia was making ravioli. He likes that.'

Hester could tell by the look on Connah's face that he was desperate to laugh, but he nodded gravely. 'We'd be delighted, Andrea. You too, of course, Luigi.'

'Alas, I cannot, I must leave soon.' Luigi beckoned his son close and, with a word of apology to the others, spoke to him at length in rapid Italian, which the boy responded to with much enthusiastic nodding.

'Don't worry, we'll take good care of him, Luigi,' said Connah.

'I have no doubt of that. I was merely telling him to behave well and to make no argument when Guido comes for him later.' Luigi bowed over Hester's hand. 'It was a great pleasure once more. I trust my son did not startle you too much.'

'No, indeed.' Hester smiled warmly at the boy, who responded in kind, his eyes sparkling. 'We'll be glad to have your company, Andrea.'

'*Grazie, signora.*'

Lowri leaned against Hester's shoulder as father and son took leave of each other, watching as Luigi hugged and kissed his son, then came to smile down at her. 'Thank you for inviting Andrea, Miss Lowri. You are very kind.'

'No problem,' she said casually. 'He can watch one of my DVDs with me after lunch, if he likes.'

'He is a very fortunate boy!' Luigi took his leave all round, embraced his son again and walked off quickly through the garden to the woods bordering his own property.

'Right then, Andrea, let's help get the lunch,' said Hester, astonishing him.

'You have no servant for that, *signora*?'

'Flavia does the cooking, but we take the tray with the knives and forks and plates and we set the table on the loggia,' said Lowri.

'*Bene*. I will help,' he assured her manfully and followed her into the kitchen, where it was plain from the ensuing flood of Italian that Flavia was shocked to have the son of *Il Conte* involved in any way with lunch other than to eat it.

'Do the boy good,' said Connah, grinning. 'While the battle rages, stroll round the garden with me, Hester, and enlighten me about the mystery that is woman.'

She laughed at him as they strolled down towards the pool. 'You mean Lowri?'

'Absolutely. One minute she's snarling at the boy, then suddenly she wants him to stay to lunch.'

'These Italian men can be very charming,' said Hester demurely.

Connah threw out his hands. 'This one's only eleven, for heaven's sake.'

'But very much a chip off the old block. And very good-looking.'

'Then why was Lowri so hostile to start with?'

'He was invading her territory. Once she made it plain that this is her patch, and he's only here on her say-so, she relented. She's sorry for him because he looked so lonely standing there when we first spotted him.' Hester grinned at him. 'Like a junior Adam expelled from Eden.'

Connah led her to a chair under one of the umbrellas. 'His arrival has one advantage. If you're worried because Lowri clings to you too much, Andrea's advent could change that. This tutor of his could give you some time off if he looks after both children now and again.'

Hester stared at him, affronted. 'Certainly not. Lowri is my responsibility.'

'Even so, it won't do any harm for this Guido to watch over them at the pool for an hour or two—talk of the devil,' Connah added, as a young man appeared through the woods. He hurried towards them with a holdall.

'*Signore, signora.*' He bowed. 'I am Guido Berni. *Il Conte* told me to bring Andrea's swimming suit.'

'Excellent,' said Connah. 'Have you brought your own?'

'*Si, signore. Il Conte* wishes me to stay to make sure Andrea is no trouble for you—if you permit.'

'We'd be delighted,' Connah assured him. 'Here comes my daughter with Andrea now.'

Andrea was not at all delighted, obviously thinking that Guido had come to fetch him home, but when the tutor explained the boy's face cleared.

'He has to stay to take me back,' he explained to Lowri, then introduced her with quaint formality to his tutor, who bowed over her hand in a way which won her over completely.

'Are you staying to lunch too?' she asked. 'It's ravioli today.'

The young man flushed with embarrassment, but Hester smiled at him reassuringly.

'Of course you must stay.'

At first Andrea was not at all happy to have his tutor included in the lunch invitation. But he brightened considerably when Connah and Hester left the younger members to their own company as they talked to Guido, who was a very likeable young man from a local Greve family.

'I am a law student at the University of Padua,' he confided, relaxing as he began to eat Flavia's unrivalled ravioli. '*Il Conte* hired me to be with Andrea during the summer vacation.'

Connah smiled as he watched Andrea listening to Lowri with rapt attention as he did his best to understand everything she said. 'He doesn't strike me as needing much tuition, unless it's to polish his English,' he commented.

'*E vero,*' said Guido with feeling. 'He is very clever. But I am not really employed to teach Andrea. He has no need of extra tuition. *Il Conte*'s need is for someone to be with his son always. As *sicurezza*—for safety, you understand.'

'Oh, yes, we understand very well,' said Hester with feeling, and the young man nodded soberly.

'Of course, with so beautiful a young daughter.'

'Exactly,' said Connah, and touched Hester's hand to forestall any explanation about relationships.

After lunch Guido sat outside on the loggia with a textbook while Lowri and Andrea watched a DVD in the shady *salone*.

Connah excused himself to do some work and Hester, suddenly at a loose end, went out to sit under an umbrella by the pool.

She would enjoy the blessed peace while she could, she decided, since her presence would be demanded in the pool once Lowri had enough of sitting still. But Hester was wrong. When Lowri came running to join her, already changed into her swimming things, she announced that Daddy said she could go in the pool with Andrea and Guido.

'We're going to play games,' she said, her eyes shining.

'Sounds good to me,' said Hester, and turned with a smile as Andrea raced to join them, with Guido following at a more sedate rate with towels and wraps.

'Will you not join us in the pool, *signora*?' asked Andrea politely.

'No, thank you. I shall be very happy to sit here and watch.'

Guido, decided Hester as she watched, was a godsend. He was not only a strong swimmer, he made up a complicated game of tag with a ball, and when the youngsters tired of that he organised races and roped in Hester as referee when there were heated arguments over the winners.

Eventually she got up and said it was time everyone got dressed and had something to drink. 'You come upstairs with me, Lowri, while Andrea and Guido change in the downstairs bathroom.'

Connah met them outside Lowri's door. 'From what I heard, you were having a wonderful time out there, *cariad*.'

Lowri beamed at him. 'It was great. Guido's so cool. Are you coming down to have tea with us?'

'Of course. I'll go down and give Flavia your orders.'

While Connah was making his request in the kitchen, Andrea, dried, dressed and sleek of hair, knocked at the door.

'Thank you for letting us use your pool, *signore*,' he said punctiliously as Guido joined them to express his own thanks.

'My pleasure,' Connah assured them. 'Now, you gentlemen can carry the trays out to the pool for Flavia.'

Flavia was so delighted to serve the son of *Il Conte* that she brought out the *torta* made for dessert for the evening meal, but when Guido and Andrea insisted on carrying the trays to the pool for her she was clearly reluctant to allow them to perform such menial tasks and only submitted when Connah advised her to accept their help.

'I'll help too,' said Lowri, running down the stairs, and Hester, coming behind, eyed Connah questioningly.

'What am I required to do?'

'Just sit under an umbrella and let us look at you,' he said in a tone which won him a searching look from his daughter.

From then on the holiday took a new turn. Next day was a repeat performance, with Andrea spending most of the day at the Casa Girasole with Guido in attendance, but Luigi Martinelli returned from Rome the day after and came early to thank Connah and Hester for being so kind to his son.

'In return, perhaps you will allow your daughter to spend time at the *Castello* today,' he suggested. 'Andrea has a little work to do this morning before he may play again. But afterwards he is most eager to have Lowri's company for the day. You need not fear. Both Guido and I will take great care of her.'

'That's very kind of you, Luigi. Lowri's upstairs, getting dressed.' Connah exchanged a look with Hester. 'Would you go up to pass on Luigi's invitation, darling?'

'Of course.' She turned to Luigi. 'Are there women servants at the Castello?'

'Yes. I promise Lowri will not lack for motherly care!' He smiled at Connah. 'And you will wish to accompany us there, to make sure you leave her in safe hands.'

Reassured, Hester went up to consult with Lowri, who, as anticipated, was wild with excitement at the idea.

'Are you coming too?' she demanded, eyes sparkling.

'No. The invitation's just for you. But Daddy's going to walk there with you and any time you want to come home, just tell Andrea's father and he'll bring you back.'

'Am I going to have lunch there?'

'Yes. So I'll put a clean T-shirt in your backpack just in case— a comb too.' Hester gave her a sudden hug. 'Have fun, darling.'

Lowri hugged her back tightly. 'I wish you were coming too.'

'Nonsense. You'll have much more fun without me.'

The child gave her a very adult look. 'I'll miss you, just the same.'

Hester swallowed a lump in her throat. 'I'll miss you too. Think how quiet it will be without you.'

But once Connah and Lowri had gone off with Luigi, the house could hardly be called quiet since Flavia was singing at the top of her voice while she whipped it into shape. After informing her, not without difficulty, that numbers were reduced for lunch, Hester learned that *Signore Connah* had already informed Flavia of this, also that she could have the rest of the day off and was leaving soon after preparing a cold supper in readiness for the evening.

'*Bene*,' said Hester, surprised, and went off to the pool with her book.

Later Flavia appeared with a coffee tray, announced that she was ready to leave and, after a cheery, '*A domani*,' she hurried into the house.

After half an hour of peaceful solitude Hester was tired of it and felt a leap of pleasure as she saw Connah emerge from the trees to take the path towards the pool. 'Was Lowri happy at being left?' she demanded.

'Couldn't wait to get rid of me,' he said, taking the chair beside her. 'Last seen climbing the tower staircase at the *Castello* with Andrea, Guido panting after them in hot pursuit.'

'I told her to tell Luigi the moment she'd had enough and wanted to come home.'

Connah chuckled as he lay back, long legs outstretched. 'It won't be any time soon.' He turned to peer under the brim of her hat, a look in his eyes which made her pulse leap. 'Has Flavia gone?'

Hester nodded silently.

'Then we're alone at last, Miss Ward.'

'Would you like some coffee?' she said, preparing to get up, but he caught her wrist.

'No coffee. Relax.'

Not easy in these circumstances, thought Hester, subsiding. 'Please don't think you have to keep me company if you have work to do.'

'I have no intention of wasting such a golden opportunity, Hester. Work can wait.'

Her mouth dried. 'Have you spoken to your mother this morning?'

'Yes. I mentioned it before I went out.'

'So you did. Sorry.'

Connah gave her a wolfish grin. 'Are you by any chance nervous now we're alone, Hester?'

She felt her colour rise. 'Of course not.'

'Then I'll just take this tray up to the house and collect a book I've been trying to finish for weeks. Don't go away.'

Hester sat very still when he'd gone. Connah was right. She was nervous—just a little. To be suddenly alone with him felt so dangerous that it took her a while to realise that her phone was ringing from the depths of her tote bag. She fished it out and eyed the caller's name in surprise.

When Connah returned a few minutes later, he looked at her with concern. 'Hester, what is it? Don't you feel well?'

'I'm fine, but I've just had a phone call.'

'From your mother?' he said quickly. 'Something wrong at home?'

'No, in Yorkshire. The call was from George Rutherford in Ilkley. His wife had a fall at the works yesterday and had to be rushed to hospital. Sarah lost the baby and she's inconsolable, poor woman. So is he.' Hester took in a deep breath and tried to smile. 'I feel horribly selfish for thinking of myself in the circumstances, when the Rutherfords are so devastated, but it means I'm out of a job. As soon as we get back I'll have to find another post.'

Connah looked down at her in silence for a moment, then held out his hand to help her up. 'I might be able to do something about that. Come inside for a while, Hester, and I'll explain.'

She took the hand, eyeing him blankly. 'You know someone who needs a Norland nanny?'

'No,' he said as they walked up the garden. 'But I know someone who needs *you*, Hester.'

'You can't mean Lowri,' she said, puzzled. 'She doesn't need a nanny any more.'

Once they reached the *salone*, Connah took her hands in his. 'I know Lowri doesn't need a nanny, exactly. But she desperately needs a woman in her life who can take care of her. And, after talking to my mother this morning, it's obvious that she can no longer take care of Lowri without help.'

Hester gazed into the eyes holding hers. 'I'm not perfectly sure what you mean.'

'You told me yourself, Hester, that Lowri would like a stepmother, and you're the perfect choice. Lowri loves you, Hester. And, unless I'm much mistaken, you feel the same about her.'

She swallowed hard, trying to control the heart that had leapt, beating wildly, to her throat. 'I do love her. But to become her stepmother—'

'You would be obliged to marry me.' He smiled crookedly. 'Is that so impossible to imagine?'

'Yes,' she said after a tense pause. 'I thought you were offering me a job.'

'I was proposing marriage, but I obviously made a hash of it.' His hands tightened on hers.

'You must love Lowri very much.'

'I do. But I care for you too. Although we met for the first time years ago, we've known each other for a relatively short time since fate brought you back into my life, but I'd miss you like hell if you left us now. You're part of our lives now, Lowri's and mine. We need you, Hester.'

She gave him a troubled look. 'But I can't forget what you said about Lowri's mother, Connah. That you never wanted to feel that way about anyone again. No marriage would stand much hope of success on those terms.'

'When the holiday's over and Lowri's back in school I'll tell you all about her mother,' he promised. 'But for now, while we have this unexpected interlude of peace and privacy, I want you to think hard about my proposal.'

As if she'd be likely to think about anything else! 'It seems a pretty drastic solution to the problem of school holidays, Connah,' she pointed out. 'When I marry I expect it to be a permanent arrangement, not some kind of business transaction that can be cancelled if it doesn't work out.'

The dark eyes hardened. 'Is that what you think I'm suggesting?'

'That's what it sounds like.' She gave him a bleak little smile. 'I must be a closet romantic after all. Much as I love Lowri— and you're perfectly right, I do love her—I can't marry you just to provide her with the stepmother she yearns for.'

'As must be patently obvious, Hester, it's not just any stepmother she yearns for. She wants you.' Connah's eyes smouldered suddenly. 'And, just so you're not in any doubt, so do I.'

CHAPTER TEN

'IS THAT so hard for you to take in?' demanded Connah, after seconds ticked away with no response from Hester.

'Yes, it is,' she said at last, when she could trust her voice. 'Did you mean it?'

His eyes lit with a disquieting gleam. 'Of course I meant it. Marrying you would obviously fulfil Lowri's need for a mother, but it would also fulfil certain needs of my own. This is no fictional marriage of convenience we're discussing. I expect it to be normal in every way.'

'That's if I agree to it,' she said, surprising him. 'I don't think you've thought this through. You don't have to resort to something as drastic as marriage, Connah. There is another solution.'

He dropped her hands abruptly. 'Explain.'

Hester stood back, her arms folded across her chest. 'When Lowri went away to school, Alice stayed on with your mother to be on hand during school holidays. You could employ me in the same way, if you think your mother might like me enough to make that feasible.'

'You'd prefer that to marrying me?' he demanded incredulously.

Of course she didn't!

'Marriage is difficult enough—so I'm told,' said Hester crisply, 'when both parties are madly in love. It's certain to be a lot more so as a mere solution to a problem.'

Connah was silent long enough to make her edgy.

'Would you have preferred me to say yes without giving a thought to the pitfalls involved?'

'Hell, yes.' He scowled, looking so much like Lowri when things went wrong that Hester's lips twitched. 'What's so funny?' he demanded.

'You looked exactly like Lowri then.'

Connah flung away to walk to the long doors leading into the garden, one hand raking his hair back as he stared out at the profusion of colour. Hester gazed at his powerful shoulders and tapering back, her eyes moving down to his long muscular legs as she wondered if she'd just made the biggest mistake of her life. Her brief encounter with him in her teens had left her dreaming about him for years. Yet now she was turning down a proposal she'd never in her wildest moment imagined in those dreams, merely because the love of her life had made it for the wrong reasons. How stupid was that? He turned round suddenly and gave her the rare, blinding smile that made nonsense of her high-flown principles. But, before she could tell him her answer was yes to anything he wanted, Connah pre-empted her.

'This is what we do, Hester. We go on with our holiday, spending time together as a family, and if by the end of it your answer's still no, I'll go with your alternative. It's not what I want, but it's a damn sight better than letting you disappear out of Lowri's life—and mine—to bring up someone else's child.' He smiled wryly. 'Though keeping you on as Mother's companion will be an extravagance. You're a lot more expensive than Alice.'

'But I'm worth it,' she said lightly, to cover her disappointment. If he really wanted to marry her, surely he could have tried a bit more persuasion.

'Oh, yes,' he said softly, 'you're worth it, Hester.'

* * *

To Hester's chagrin, Connah kept very firmly to his plan for the rest of the holiday. Lowri spent some days with Andrea at the *Castello*, which meant that Hester was often alone with Connah for hours at a time. But, although he constantly reminded her in unspoken, subtle ways that their relationship had changed, he never took advantage of their time alone together to plead his cause. Which served her right, she thought irritably. Connah had said this was what they'd do, and that was that.

From then on Hester's underlying tension, far from spoiling her holiday, merely added a *frisson* of excitement to both the tranquil lazy days and the various expeditions to explore Tuscany. These outings were usually planned for the days when Flavia's husband Nico came to augment his job at the *Castello* by working in the garden at Casa Girasole. On one of Nico's days they were invited to lunch at the *Castello* and, because Guido had been given time off to visit his family, Connah remained with the children in the gardens while Hester accompanied their host on a brief tour of the turrets and towers of his ancient mediaeval home, marvelling that it was in such excellent repair.

'Since it was her reason for marrying me,' said Luigi, 'my wife considers her dowry well spent on maintenance of the *Castello*.'

Hester smiled at her spectacularly handsome host. 'I can't believe it was her only reason.'

He bowed, smiling cynically. 'At the time, possibly not, but it is the only reason which now survives. Are you going to marry Connah?' he added abruptly. 'He behaves like the dog with the bone over you. I am amazed he allowed you to tour my home alone with me.'

'I don't care for the word *allow*,' said Hester without heat, and he smiled ruefully.

'Forgive me. I do not express myself well in your language.'

She laughed. 'I think you do it very well.'

Again the bow. '*Mille grazie*, Hester. Now, let us join Connah before he comes to murder me.'

On one level it was a truly glorious holiday, with day trips to the ancient towers of San Gimignano and the great fan-shaped square of Siena and, last but not least, a triumphantly successful outing to Florence. After queuing to marvel at Michelangelo's David in the Accademia, they went on a tour of the wonderful shops before settling down to a long, lazy lunch. Lowri liked this outing best of all because Andrea went with them, which gave her a lot to write about on the postcards she sent off at regular intervals. But she wrote sealed letters to Chloe, Hester noted, amused. Detailed information about Andrea was obviously not to be trusted to a postcard anyone could read.

But on another level the holiday was a subtle waiting game that Connah indicated very plainly he intended to win.

The day before they were due to fly home, Andrea invited Lowri to a farewell lunch at the *Castello*. Connah walked there with her in the morning and then stayed to drink coffee with Luigi while Hester remained at the villa to finish off as much packing as possible. The house was more peaceful than usual because Flavia had been given the day off to make up for the extra hours she would put in after they left to prepare the house for the next visit of the Andersons.

Satisfied that the packing was complete other than last minute additions, Hester laid the table outside, then settled down there with the last of her supply of books. But she soon gave up trying to read and just sat, gazing out at the sunlit vista of flower-filled garden and the pool and hills beyond. She sighed, depressed. It would probably be raining when they got home tomorrow and life would return to normal, whatever normal might be in future. Back in Albany Square, Connah might even revert to remote employer again for the short time before Lowri went back to school.

'Why are you scowling?'

Hester looked up, startled, to find Connah standing over her. 'I didn't notice you coming through the garden.'

'I walked back via the village to post Lowri's letter.' He raked his dark hair back from his sweating forehead. 'Mad idea at this time of day. I need a drink. Can I get you one?'

She shook her head. 'I'll come in now to start lunch.'

'Then I'll sit at the kitchen table and watch.'

Hester put a pan of water to heat for the pasta and lit a low flame under the sauce Flavia had left ready the day before. Connah settled at the kitchen table with a bottle of mineral water, long legs outstretched, his eyes following every move while she put the simple meal together.

'If you need to wash, this will be ready in five minutes,' Hester told him, her tone tart because her fingers had turned to thumbs under the intent dark gaze.

'Yes, Nanny,' he mocked and retired to the ground floor bathroom.

She looked after him, biting her lip. His walk had put him in an odd mood. Which was a pity, when this would be their last lunch alone together. At least it would taste good. She drained the pasta, poured hot sauce over it and, because her appetite had taken a sudden nosedive, gave Connah the lion's share. She carried the tray out to the loggia, determined to be pleasant and conversational even if it choked her.

'That smells good,' said Connah as she set a bowl in front of him.

She nodded. 'I'll miss Flavia's cooking when we get back.'

'Yours is equally good, Hester.'

'Thank you. How was Lowri when you left?'

'About to embark on a treasure hunt in the *Castello* with Andrea, armed with clues in verse composed in two languages by Guido—a young man of many talents.' Connah smiled at her as he twirled his fork expertly in his pasta. 'Life will seem so flat for Lowri in Albany Square. I'll take her to visit my mother as soon as we get back so she can brag to Owen about her holiday.'

Hester smiled. 'She bought him a belt in Florence. Is he the kind of boy who'll appreciate something like that?'

Connah nodded. 'He's a good kid. Even if he doesn't like it, he'll thank her politely. Grandma Griffiths brought him up well. But if he's been told about Alice's baby he'll be able to trump Lowri's holiday news pretty effectively.'

Hester was finding it easier to sip water than eat, and Connah noticed. He noticed everything, she thought crossly.

'Aren't you hungry, Hester?' he asked, so gently she had a sudden, absurd desire to cry.

She smiled at him instead. 'Not terribly. It's so hot today.'

He poured her a glass of wine. 'Have some of this, then.'

Hester rarely drank wine at lunch time because it made her drowsy in the heat. But she fancied it just this once, she thought morosely. Afterwards she'd go up to her room for a nap. She would take her book to bed and doze the time away until Connah fetched his daughter home—because home for Lowri meant Connah. Something Hester could relate to all too easily.

'That's a strange look, Hester,' said Connah.

'The house is always so quiet without Lowri.'

'Peaceful, rather.' He looked at her bowl. 'You haven't eaten much.'

'No.' She got up to put the dishes on the tray. 'I'll just put these in the dishwasher, then I'll go up to read on my bed for a while.'

'No coffee?'

'Not for me, but I'll make some for you—'

'No.' He took the tray from her. 'I'll see to these.'

Hester thanked him very formally and went up to her room, deliberately depriving herself of a post-lunch hour alone with Connah. It was only prolonging the agony, she thought bitterly.

It was almost the end of the holiday and he'd made no actual reference to the proposal again. The days of lotus-eating at the Casa Girasole were over.

Hester stretched out on the bed in her cool, airy room and watched the filmy white curtains moving slightly in the faint warm breeze as she wondered what Lowri was doing right now. But, between them, Luigi and Guido would see that she came to no harm.

Quite sure that she'd lie awake all afternoon, Hester dozed a little eventually, but woke with a start to see Connah leaning in the open doorway, his lean torso and long legs tanned by this time to a shade of bronze which contrasted darkly with the white towel slung round his hips. Her stomach muscles tightened at the look in his eyes as he lounged away from the lintel and strolled towards the bed.

'This has gone on long enough, Hester.' He stood looking down at her in silence, a pulse throbbing at the corner of his mouth. Slowly he put a knee on the edge of the bed and leaned over her, his eyes smouldering down into hers for a second before he took her mouth with a kiss that made her head reel.

'Weeks ago you seemed to doubt that I wanted you,' he said in a tone which sent fire streaking down her spine as he pulled her against him. 'It's time you learned that I meant it.'

Held so close to him that she had trouble breathing, Hester knew very well that he wanted her. But, much as her body urged her to, she wasn't ready to surrender that easily. Summoning every last scrap of self-control, she pushed at him until her hands, flat against his chest, held him away a fraction.

'You're teaching me a lesson?' she demanded unevenly.

Connah flicked her hands away and pulled her close again. 'A lesson in love,' he whispered and kissed her again with a heat and passion intended to remove all possible doubt. When he raised his head at last his eyes glittered in triumphant possession as he tossed the sheet aside to look at her.

Hester felt her entire body grow taut in response to the eyes which moved over her in a scrutiny as tactile as a long drawn out caress. At last he pulled her into his arms, his mouth possessing hers with such fierce tenderness that everything was suddenly simple. He wanted her. And she wanted him. It was utterly pointless to pretend otherwise. She wreathed her hands round his neck, responding hotly to his lips and tongue and subtle, provoking hands. One of them slid into her hair to hold her head back as his mouth slid down her throat to linger on the throbbing pulse there, before it continued on a tantalisingly slow journey downward, tasting every inch of her before his mouth closed on each nipple in turn, his grazing teeth sending darts of fire to melt her into hot, liquid response. He uttered a growl of pure male satisfaction as his exploring fingers discovered her readiness, causing turbulence which mounted to fever pitch when his tongue replaced them. She went wild as he caressed the taut little bud he found with unerring aim. She gasped, her hair tossing back and forth on the pillows until he gave in to the demand of her frenzied hands on his shoulders and slid up over her and inside her to rocket them both on a tumultuous race with an engulfing, shattering orgasm as the prize.

Before Hester could even breathe normally again, Connah heaved himself up on his hands to look down into her stunned eyes. 'Are you angry?' he panted.

'Not—angry,' she gasped. Shattered in several pieces, possibly, but not angry.

'Good,' said Connah with satisfaction, and let himself down beside her. 'That means I won.'

Her eyes narrowed as she fought to breathe normally. 'Won what?'

'My gamble. I took a chance that this was the right way to convince you that we'd be good together. Not just good—spectacular,' he amended, kissing her swiftly. 'But it was a risk. I could have alienated you completely.'

She surveyed him, narrow-eyed. 'It's quite obvious that you won. You must have noticed I'm not complaining.'

He stared at her. 'Hester, you could have said no at any stage—'

'Oh, I know that,' she said impatiently. 'I meant there was no need for your gamble. If you hadn't insisted on your plan, I would have said yes long ago.'

Connah's eyes narrowed in menace. 'You mean you've kept me on a string all this time as some kind of dressage?'

'Certainly not. You made the rules. I kept to them,' she said sweetly.

He laughed and pulled her into his arms. 'So you'll marry me, then.'

Her lips twitched. 'You could try phrasing it a little more gracefully!'

He looked deep into her eyes for a long, sober moment. 'Will you do me the honour of becoming my wife, Miss Ward? I strongly advise you to say yes. If you don't, I'll keep you here in this bed until you do.'

Did he really doubt her answer? Hester pretended to think it over. 'Since it's nearly time for you to fetch Lowri home, I don't have much choice. So the answer's yes, Mr Carey Jones, I will.'

'Good,' he said with satisfaction. 'We'll get married right away.'

She blinked. 'Why the rush?'

His eyes gleamed implacably. 'I want it signed and sealed as soon as possible.'

Hester pushed him away and sat up, pulling the sheet up to her chin. 'Why, Connah?'

'Because, once having set something in motion, I like to see it through to completion with all possible speed.' He shrugged. 'I'm no good at flowery speeches, Hester, but I'm deeply grateful to you for taking Lowri and me on for life. Because that's what saying yes means. You do understand that?'

'Perfectly,' she assured him.

He eased her back down beside him. 'You said that respect and rapport were your main requirements in a relationship and, God knows, I respect you, Hester. I also like you enormously and enjoy your company, and I felt a strong rapport with you from the first moment we met up again. Now we've proved beyond all doubt that it's physical as well as mental, we have the basis for a very successful marriage.'

Not quite, thought Hester, her face buried against his shoulder. One major emotion was missing from his list. But she'd known that in advance. His capacity for love had been expended on Lowri's mother. But she was dead, poor lady, while Hester Ward was not only very much alive, but fiercely determined that Connah's feelings for her would eventually change into something a whole lot hotter than mere liking and respect.

She raised her head as she felt his body tense. 'What's the matter?'

Connah rubbed his cheek against hers. 'The magnitude of the risk just struck me.'

Hester eyed him curiously. 'Risk?'

'How would I have faced Lowri if you'd refused to come back to Albany Square with us?'

'I wouldn't have hurt Lowri by refusing to do that.'

He raised a sardonic eyebrow. 'Wouldn't you care about hurting me?'

'I hope,' she said primly, 'that I'd care about hurting anyone. But this is all hypothetical so it doesn't apply. You won your gamble.'

'In the most ravishing way possible!' He kissed her again, then sat up with a heavy sigh. 'If I didn't have to fetch Lowri we could repeat the experience, just to make sure.'

'Sure of what?'

'That you're completely clear on what I expect from our

marriage.' He reached for the discarded towel, then turned to look down at her.

'Not quite, Connah. Could you clarify things a little more?' she said demurely and smiled at him, her eyes dancing.

His eyes blazed in response as he reached for her phone.

'Luigi? Would you mind keeping Lowri a little longer? I've got something I need to see to here before I fetch her.' He paused. 'Wonderful. In an hour, then. *Grazie*.'

He dived back into bed, laughing against Hester's open mouth as he began making love to her all over again, this time with such slow, tormenting attention to every part of her that the hour was almost up before Connah could force himself to get out of bed.

'I need a shower,' he said, kissing her, and grinned. 'If I wasn't pushed for time, I'd suggest we had one together.'

Hester smiled drowsily. 'I'll take a rain check.'

Connah bent to touch a finger to her bottom lip. 'I'll remind you of that soon. Very soon. Ciao.'

Hester lay where she was for a minute or two, pinched herself to make sure she hadn't been dreaming, and went into the bathroom for a shower which she took, not without regret, on her own. As she dried herself she studied herself in the steamy mirror, trying to be objective about it. Whatever his motives for asking her to marry him, Connah had proved beyond all doubt that physically he found her desirable. He also said he liked her, respected her and enjoyed her company. She pointed an imperious finger at her reflection. Now, she told it, you just need him to fall madly in love with you.

When Lowri arrived home she was in a bubbling mood as she described the treasure hunt. 'Andrea was quite sad when I said goodbye,' she said over supper on the loggia. 'He asked me to come back again. Can we come back some time, Daddy?' she asked.

'Quite possibly, if the Andersons will let us. We can't stay longer right now because they're coming here themselves next week.' Connah smiled. 'It is their house, *cariad.*'

'Andrea said we could stay at the *Castello* next time.'

'Would you like that?' asked Hester.

Lowri thought about it. 'I'm not sure. It's so *old!* It's great to play in but it might be a bit creepy at night. I'd rather stay here. Besides, we've got a pool here and there's only that crumbly old fountain with Neptune and the mermaids at the *Castello.*'

She chattered all through the meal and her favourite *panacotta* which followed it, then looked at her father in question as he reached out a hand to take hers.

'Lowri, we have some very special news for you.'

She eyed him with deep misgiving. 'Bad news?'

Connah smiled at her lovingly. 'No, *cariad.* It's very good news. While you were out this afternoon I asked Hester to marry me and she said yes.'

Lowri's mouth opened almost as wide as her blue eyes. She looked wildly from her father to Hester. 'You really, really mean it?'

'Would I joke about a thing like that?' said Connah lovingly.

Lowri jumped to her feet and hurled herself at Hester, tears pouring down her face. 'You're going to live with us forever and ever?'

'Yes, darling,' said Hester huskily and held the child close. 'Are you pleased?'

The child nodded vehemently, burrowing her face into Hester's shoulder. She looked up, her eyes shining like stars in her wet face. 'Does that mean I'll get a baby sister as well?'

Hester's face burned as a pair of amused black eyes met hers over Lowri's head. 'Maybe, one day.'

Lowri whirled round to face her father. 'Hester must come with us to see Grandma when we go back, then I can take her to meet Owen and Alice.'

'How do you feel about that, Hester?' asked Connah.

'I think you and Lowri should go to Bryn Derwen on your own first, while I visit my mother and Robert,' said Hester and smiled wryly. 'You can break the news to your mother gently, Connah, and I'll come with you next time.'

'Don't worry, Hester, Grandma will be pleased,' Lowri assured her. 'She's always telling Daddy he should get a wife.'

'And, being a dutiful son,' Connah said, smiling smugly, 'I've done my best to please her. I assume,' he added, hugging his daughter, 'that you're pleased, too.'

Lowri hugged him back as hard as she could. 'I never thought I'd be so lucky.'

'Neither did I,' he told her, meeting Hester's eyes over the shining dark head.

CHAPTER ELEVEN

DURING the flight home Lowri talked non-stop about the wedding, her face glowing with excitement.

'Can I be bridesmaid?' she asked at one stage.

'Yes, of course, but I'd like a very simple wedding,' said Hester quickly. There had probably been a grand affair first time round, with all the usual attendant fuss, and Connah would naturally want something very different for a second marriage. 'My mother and Robert had a private ceremony with just a few friends. I'd like the same.'

'But you can still be bridesmaid, *cariad*,' said Connah, as Lowri's face fell.

'With a puffy dress too,' added Hester.

'Perfect!' Lowri said, relieved, then smiled rapturously. 'Can I tell Sam?'

Since he was waiting for them at Heathrow, Lowri was able to tell him soon after they landed.

'And just as well,' murmured Connah as his daughter flew towards Sam. 'Otherwise she might have exploded.'

'Will you break the news to your mother first, before driving to see her?'

'No. I'll make sure she's feeling well before I spring any surprises. Lowri will just have to contain herself until I say the word.'

Connah smiled as Lowri came skipping back with Sam as he hurried to welcome them home. 'How are things in Albany Square?'

'No problems, Boss.' Sam grinned from ear to ear. 'Lowri's just told me the news. My sincere congratulations to you both.'

'Thank you.' Connah shook his proffered hand. 'It took some persuasion, but Hester finally said yes.'

Sam smiled at her warmly. 'I hope you'll both be very happy. Best news I've had in a long time.'

'Thank you, Sam.'

'Sam, Hester's going to be my stepmother,' Lowri broke in, beaming. 'And maybe one day—'

'Time we were on our way,' said Hester quickly, avoiding Connah's eye.

They had barely left the airport for the motorway before the combined effect of Lowri's excitement and a restless night sent her to sleep. Connah smiled over his shoulder at Hester. 'Out for the count?' he asked softly.

She nodded, shifting the child more comfortably against her shoulder. She hadn't slept much herself. After a brief doze towards dawn, she'd sat up suddenly, wondering if she'd dreamt it all. And had felt a great glow of happiness when she'd realised it was all true. But the glow dimmed slightly when Connah told Sam to drive Hester to her parents' house next morning.

'I'm taking off with Lowri to Bryn Derwen first thing, so I'll leave it to you to see Hester's delivered safely.'

'Right you are, Boss.'

Reluctant to wake Lowri, Hester postponed her protests until Lowri was in bed that night.

'I can walk home tomorrow,' she told Connah when she joined him in the study. 'I'll leave in the morning soon after you do, and I'll be back the same time the next day.'

'Indulge me, Hester,' said Connah, 'I'll feel a damn sight happier if Sam drives you there.' He drew her down beside him.

'Now, let's talk. Where would you like to go for our honey-moon? Paris? Bali? Blackpool?'

Hester chuckled, diverted, and gave it some thought. 'I suppose we couldn't go back to the Casa Girasole?'

'I can ask Jay. Is that what you want?'

'It's what I'd like.'

'Then I shall enquire.' He gave her a look that clenched certain inner muscles in response. 'But Flavia would have to come in a lot later in the mornings.'

'Would she have to come in at all?'

'I suppose I can always pay her the same money and tell her to take a holiday. For my part, I don't much mind where we go. Privacy is my priority.'

Hester looked at him steadily. 'Mine is a different place from your first honeymoon.'

Connah's eyes shuttered. 'When I come back from Bryn Derwen I'll tell you everything,' he promised. 'But right now I refuse to let the past encroach on the happier present. Talking of which, I must buy you a ring.'

Hester shook her head. 'A wedding ring at the appropriate time will do, Connah.'

He pulled her on to his lap so abruptly that she stared at him, startled. Back here in the formality of Albany Square, the sudden intimacy was unexpected. 'We'll go shopping when I come back,' he said with emphasis. 'Just in case you need reminding, Hester, this is to be a normal marriage in every way, including a short—very short—preceding engagement. Complete with ring.' He kissed her very thoroughly by way of emphasis.

Startled, thrilled, her veins humming with the response Connah's slightest touch aroused in her since he'd made love to her, Hester thanked him, her voice not quite steady. 'It's just that I'd hate you to think I was in any way mercenary.'

Connah gave her the smile which always turned her into a not-quite-set jelly. 'You mean you're not marrying me for my money? Why, then?'

Other than getting her heart's desire? Hester thought about it. 'Various reasons,' she said at last.

'One of them, I assume, is my daughter.'

'Since I wouldn't be working for you without her, yes.'

Connah nodded. 'And the other reasons?'

'The same as yours, more or less.'

'You mean rapport, respect and mind-blowing sex?'

Hester gave an involuntary crow of laughter which Connah smothered with a kiss.

'I suppose there's no hope of the last part tonight?' he whispered against her lips.

'Absolutely not!'

'When, then?'

Hester gave him a long look. 'I'd rather wait to actually sleep with you until we're married. Or at least until Lowri goes back to school.'

Connah's heavy eyelids lowered over a calculating gleam. 'Who said anything about sleep?' He eyed her in silence for a moment, then sighed heavily. 'You mean it.'

'Yes. Not because I don't want to.' She gave him a swift kiss so passionate that his grip on her waist tightened painfully. 'But Lowri might find it odd if I suddenly changed bedrooms.'

Connah smiled wryly. 'And God knows I want my daughter to be happy. But I'm going to do my damnedest to make sure you're happy too, Hester.'

'I hope to do the same for you, Connah,' she said soberly. 'I'll certainly try.'

'You don't have to try.' He tilted her face up to his. 'But if you won't sleep with me, a few more kisses like that one would make me happy for the time being. The very first kiss you've given me of your own accord, incidentally.'

'I don't go round kissing my employers,' she said severely.

'Not even the baby-faced actor?'

'Keir wasn't my employer.'

Next morning Hester kissed an excited, bubbling Lowri goodbye, then lifted her face for the kiss Connah took his time over, to his daughter's deep satisfaction.

'Give my regards to your mother and Robert,' he said as he got in the car. 'We'll have them over for dinner as soon as I get back. And let Sam drive you. Please,' he added, with an intense black look of something so much more entreaty than command that Hester gave in.

'I will, Connah.'

'I'll ring you tonight,' called Lowri as the car began to move. 'I expect Daddy will too.'

'Count on it,' said Connah.

Hester stayed where she was for a moment, feeling oddly forlorn as she watched the car glide away down the access road. She shook herself impatiently and went up into the house to see Sam. 'I'd like to leave in about ten minutes, if that's all right with you. Though I'd much rather walk.'

Sam nodded. 'I know you would. But Connah wants me to drive you there, so that's what I'll do.'

'You too, Sam?' she demanded. 'Is there something I'm not being told?'

'Connah doesn't confide in me, Hester.'

She sighed, defeated. 'OK. I'll be down shortly.'

Sam drove her to Hill Cottage, but tactfully turned down Moira's offer of coffee and promised to return the next morning to take Hester back to Albany Square. Moira and Robert hurried Hester through the house into the garden, demanding every detail of the holiday.

'Lowri was sweet, sending us so many postcards,' said Moira. 'She obviously had a wonderful time.'

'I think you did too, Hester,' said Robert, eyeing her glowing face.

She nodded happily. 'The best.'

They lingered over coffee in the garden, taking advantage of the weather, which was forecast to change later in the day. Hester handed over their presents, then sat back smiling as her mother exclaimed over the glove soft leather handbag bought in Florence, Robert equally delighted with his wallet from the same source.

'You were so extravagant, darling,' said Moira, 'but it's a gorgeous bag—I just love it.'

'Right,' said Hester, bracing herself. 'Now you're sitting comfortably, I have some news to give you. Some bad, some good.'

Moira braced herself. 'The bad news first then, please.'

'Mr Rutherford rang me while I was in Italy. His wife had a fall and lost the baby.'

'Oh poor *girl*! How is she?'

'Still desperately upset when I rang last night. I feel so sorry for her.'

'That means you don't have another job lined up yet,' said Robert, cutting straight to the chase.

'No. But here's the good news.' Hester took in a deep breath and smiled shakily. 'Connah's asked me to marry him. And I've said yes.'

Moira stared at her daughter in blank astonishment. 'I can't believe it!'

'I can, easily,' said Robert, surprising his wife even more. 'I had a feeling the wind was blowing that way when Connah drove here to collect Hester.'

'Well, I didn't. My maternal radar failed on that one.' Moira got up to clasp her daughter in a rib-cracking embrace. 'Are you really, truly happy about this, darling?'

'Really, truly,' Hester assured her. 'And Lowri is ecstatic.'

'More to the point, is Connah ecstatic too?' said Robert.

Hester smiled demurely. 'He seems to be.'

'So you're not just a mother for Lowri?' said Moira anxiously.

'No. Connah wants to marry me for the usual reasons.'

'You mean he's in love with you?'

'Not yet.' Hester gave her the details of Connah's recipe for a successful marriage.

'That's all very well,' said Moira, frowning, as she sat down again. 'But to make a marriage work you need rather more than liking and respect, rapport or not.'

Hester coloured slightly. 'The "rather more" isn't missing, Mother.'

'You mean he's physically attracted to you,' said Robert, nodding sagely.

'But do you feel the same about him?' demanded Moira.

Hester gave her mother a wry little smile. 'You know perfectly well that I fell head over heels the first time I saw him. But he belonged to somebody else then—'

'And you were very young!'

'Old enough to dream about him for ages. I just couldn't get him out of my head,' admitted Hester ruefully. 'When he walked into his study the day of my interview and I was actually face to face with my dream lover at last, I realised why no other man in my life had ever measured up to him. And if I didn't feel like that, liking and rapport or not, I wouldn't marry him.'

'Thank God for that,' said Moira, relieved. 'Has he talked about Lowri's mother yet?'

'No. Connah's leaving that until he gets back from Bryn Derwen.'

'But you think he still loves her?'

'I know he does.' Hester looked her mother in the eye. 'But I can live with that.'

* * *

Lowri rang after lunch to say they'd arrived safely, and Grandma was looking a little better. 'Daddy's taking me to the farm to see Owen so I can't talk for long. But I wish you'd come with us, Hester.'

'I will next time.'

'Give my love to your Mummy and Robert. Daddy says he'll ring you tonight about ten.'

Soon after the celebration dinner Moira had insisted on cooking, Hester pleaded weariness and went outside to climb the steps to her own room to wait, knowing, or at least hoping, that Connah would be punctual.

'Where are you?' he asked on the stroke of ten.

'Alone in my retreat. Where are you?'

'In the garden. Next time, I want you here with me, Hester. My mother's anxious to meet you. She's very pleased, by the way.'

'I'm glad. How is she?'

'Better, though still fragile. But the news that I'm getting married at last cheered her enormously. I think a big part of her problem in getting well was her worry over Lowri.'

'I do hope she'll like me.' But I want *you* to love me desperately, thought Hester and bit her lip, half afraid she'd spoken aloud, but, since Connah assured her that his mother would very definitely like her, assumed she had not.

'Lowri missed you today. So did I,' he added, his voice a tone lower.

Not sure how to respond to that, Hester asked about the visit to the farm. 'Did Owen like his belt?'

'Surprisingly, he was delighted—as much by Lowri buying him a present, I think, as the actual belt.'

'And how's Alice?'

'Blooming, very round, and very happy. Owen, by the way, is tickled pink at the prospect of a baby, so is Mal. But Lowri is so full of herself over having you for a stepmother, she wasn't as envious as she might have been. *Did* you miss me, Hester?' he added.

'Yes.' After four sun-drenched weeks spent almost constantly in Connah's company, Hester had missed him badly. 'I wish you could have been there to share the special dinner Mother whipped up. Robert produced some vintage champagne to mark the occasion.'

'Sorry I missed it. They were happy with your news?'

'Yes, once they were sure that I'm happy too.'

'I'll make an official visit as soon as I get back. With Lowri, of course. You can keep her occupied while I ask your parents' blessing.'

'No problem there. Do we have your mother's blessing too?'

'Very much so. With one reservation. She thinks I should have told you everything about Lowri's mother before asking you to marry me.'

'Why?'

'Once Lowri's in bed tomorrow night I'll explain, I promise. Now, tell me again that you miss me,' he added softly.

'I do. Desperately. I wish you were here with me right now.'

'I'll remind you of that tomorrow night, Hester!' he said, a note in his voice which curled her bare toes.

Sam arrived promptly at eleven the next morning. This time he accepted the offer of coffee and stayed chatting for a while with the Marshalls before driving Hester back to Albany Square.

'Your parents are obviously pleased for you,' he commented as they set off.

'They were—once they got over the surprise.'

'They're giving you into safe hands. Connah's a good man.' Sam shot her a sidelong grin. 'And damn lucky too, to get a wife like you at last.'

'Thank you.' Since meeting him again, it had astonished

Hester that a man like Connah was still single, but she had no intention of asking Sam if he knew why.

'Should I be doing some food shopping?' she asked as Sam turned into the garage.

'Not today. I've ordered enough in for the time being.'

As Hester got out she gave a smothered screech as a man rushed towards her from the open garage doorway.

'Please,' he said urgently. 'I need to talk to you—'

'Like hell you do!' Sam blocked his way, glaring at him.

A pair of angry blue eyes glared back. 'I wasn't talking to you. I just wanted a word with this lady.'

'Only after you deal with me,' snapped Sam. 'Name, please, or we call the police.'

The man stood his ground. 'That won't be necessary,' he said coldly. 'My name is Peter Lang, I'm a university lecturer and I'm here in town on a visit to my sister.'

'But why do you want to speak to me?' asked Hester as her heart resumed its normal beat.

He turned to her in appeal, pointedly ignoring Sam. 'I hoped you might give me some information.'

'What kind of information?' she asked, frowning.

'About the little girl in the park.'

Sam's face shut like a steel trap. 'Get the police, Hester.'

'For God's sake,' said the man, incensed. 'I'm not interested in her that way! I spoke to her because the child reminded me of someone I once knew. She told me that this lady isn't her mother, but—'

'For your information, Mr Lang, Miss Ward is the fiancée of the owner of this property,' said Sam brusquely.

'I see.' He reached into his breast pocket and handed his wallet to Sam. 'To confirm my ID,' he said, and looked at Hester. 'If I frightened the child, I apologise sincerely. I meant no harm.'

'As it happens, you didn't frighten her,' Hester informed him coldly. 'She'd been forewarned in school about men like you.'

His pallor deepened. 'I am not a paedophile,' he said through his teeth. 'I just want to contact her mother before I fly back.'

'If you want any information, I suggest you apply to my fiancé,' said Hester.

Their visitor nodded numbly. 'When would be a good time?'

Sam glanced at his watch. 'He'll be here soon. You'd better come up to my place and wait.'

When they reached his quarters, Sam glanced at one of the monitors. 'My boss has just arrived. Wait here, Mr Lang, while I talk to him.'

Sam ushered Hester out swiftly and shut his door a split second before Lowri came running up to throw herself into Hester's arms.

'Daddy said you'd be here.'

'Of course I am.' Hester hugged her close. 'Where else would I be?' She smiled up at Connah as he reached the head of the stairs. 'You're early.'

'Some of us were impatient to get away,' he said wryly. 'My intention was to stop for a snack on the way, but madam here wouldn't go for that. She wanted to get back to you.'

'Right,' said Hester, exchanging a look with Sam. 'I'll take Lowri up to her room to put her things away.'

'Could I have a private word, Boss?' said Sam.

Connah shot a searching look at him, then raised an eyebrow at Hester, but she touched a surreptitious finger to her lip and took Lowri off to ask about the visit to Grandma and the farm. Lowri was only too happy to oblige. Hester had been given every last detail when, after what seemed like hours, Connah finally rang her.

'Come down to the study, please, Hester,' said Connah in a tone which made her shiver. 'Sam will stay with Lowri for a while.'

'Daddy wants me downstairs,' Hester told Lowri. 'So Sam will come up here in a minute to keep you company. You can show him all your photographs again.'

'Why can't I come down too?'

'Daddy has a visitor he wants me to meet. I'll be back as soon as I can.'

Hester ran downstairs to find Sam waiting for her outside the study. 'Is Mr Lang still here?'

'No, he just left. The boss is waiting for you,' he said, and started upstairs. 'I'll go and see Lowri.'

Connah was standing in front of the empty fireplace and one look at his face filled Hester with dread.

'What's wrong?' she asked fearfully. 'Did you speak to this Mr Lang?'

'Yes. Come and sit down.'

She sat on the edge of one of the sofas, eyeing him with deep misgiving. 'Are you going to sit beside me?'

'No. I'll do better on my feet,' he said tersely, and ran a hand through his hair. 'My mother was right, as usual. I should have told you this before I asked you to marry me.'

'Is it something to do with Mr Lang?'

'Yes.' He paused, as though searching for the words to say next. 'There's no easy way to put this. Peter Lang is Lowri's father.'

Hester stared at him in total shock. 'I don't understand,' she said at last. 'If he was your wife's lover—'

'Laura was my twin sister, not my wife.' His face contorted suddenly. 'God knows how I managed to stop myself from strangling that man just now.'

'So Lowri's your niece,' Hester said slowly.

'Not to me. In every way other than biologically she's my daughter,' he said flatly. 'After Laura died giving birth to her, I adopted Lowri legally.'

'Welsh for Laura,' murmured Hester in sudden comprehension. 'So that's why you're so careful about Lowri's safety. You're afraid Peter Lang will take her away from you.'

'Just let him try!' said Connah fiercely, then shrugged. 'But he won't because he doesn't know he's her father. He never knew that Laura was pregnant.'

'So what did you tell Mr Lang?'

'That Laura was dead.'

'Nothing else?'

'Nothing.' Connah's eyes glittered coldly. 'He met Laura when he first started lecturing at Brown and she was at the British Embassy in Boston. They became lovers almost from the first and the inevitable happened.' His mouth twisted. 'But, before she could give her lover the glad news that she was pregnant, she discovered, due to a guest list she was compiling for some embassy function, that Peter Lang had a wife he'd forgotten to mention. Utterly heartbroken, she told her boss she was needed at home and caught the first flight available to Heathrow. I met her at the airport the night I knocked on your mother's door.' The bleak look in his eyes cut Hester to the heart.

'She was in the other room. I never saw her,' she said softly.

'She hadn't eaten or slept in days, so she was in such bad shape by the time we got to your house that I put her straight to bed. And, as you know, your wonderful mother let us stay until Laura was able to travel home with me to Norfolk.'

'Did Peter Lang try to contact her?'

'Yes, he was a nuisance. He bombarded Laura with telephone calls for a while. When she refused to speak to him, he flew over and went to the house, but Laura refused to see him either, because her condition was obvious by then. To give him his due, Lang made several more attempts to see her before he finally gave up and flew back to the States. After that he resorted to letters, telling her he was getting a divorce so they could marry. After the first one she returned the rest unopened. Laura saw

things in black and white. The love of her life had deliberately
deceived her and she couldn't forgive that. Laura was in a pretty
low state physically as well as mentally and caught every bug
going the rounds during the pregnancy. The final straw was pneu-
monia. The baby arrived a month early and, tiny though she was,
survived. Laura did not.' Connah's face contorted with pain at
the memory.

'I'm so deeply sorry,' said Hester, her heart wrung. 'When did
your mother move to Bryn Derwen?'

'She'd always wanted to return to the part of Wales she came
from, so I bought the house months before the baby was due. My
intention was to move all three of them there after the birth, to
give Laura a fresh start. But in the end my mother took the baby
there on her own, engaged a nice, kind girl from the local village
to help look after the child officially known as my daughter, and
you know the rest.' He shrugged. 'Due to my success in the financial world, I've always been security conscious. But when I
heard that some man was sniffing round Lowri alarm bells rang.'

'Why was Peter Lang here in town?'

'By some ironic twist of fate, he is working over here at the
moment. But he flies back to America next week, ready for the
start of the autumn term.'

'Unaware that he has a beautiful daughter,' said Hester
thoughtfully.

Connah gave her a searing look. 'Are you implying that I
should tell him?'

'That's entirely your decision. But I wish you'd told me.'

'Would you have turned me down if you'd known?'

'No—'

'Then I don't see what difference it makes.'

'The difference is that you didn't trust me with the truth,' said
Hester bleakly. 'You left trust out of your blueprint for a successful marriage.'

'Of course I trust you,' he said impatiently. 'Enough to know that Lowri's happiness means a damn sight more to you than Lang's.'

'Are you going to tell her the truth one day?'

'I suppose I must.' Connah rubbed his eyes wearily. 'Probably when she first needs a birth certificate, which states that her mother was Laura Carey Jones, father unknown. But by that time she should be old enough to cope with the truth.' He opened his eyes to look at Hester. 'You're not happy with this.'

'No.' She got up. 'But don't worry, I'll do my best to put on an act. Lowri is so happy that I just can't let her think something is wrong.'

Connah caught her hand with sudden urgency. 'Has this changed your mind about marrying me?'

Hester shook her head silently.

'Because of my daughter?' he demanded.

'Partly,' she said honestly. 'If it wasn't for Lowry, I'd suggest we slowed down, backtracked a little. But—'

'But, because of Lowri, you'll keep your word.'

'I always keep my word,' she retorted. 'I was going to say that if it wasn't for Lowri, the entire question wouldn't have arisen. You're marrying me to get a mother for her—'

'And to provide a wife for myself, Hester. Don't forget that,' he said harshly.

'No,' she said wearily. 'I won't.'

'Good.' Connah released her hand, eyeing her in a way which put her on guard. 'But, before we leave the subject, I need your word that you'll never contact Lang to tell him the truth.'

She gave him a hostile stare, feeling as though a lump of ice had lodged in her chest. 'You really had to ask me that?' She flung up her right hand. 'All right. I swear I will never contact Peter Lang for any reason whatsoever, so help me God.'

'Hester.' Connah started towards her, but she turned her back on him and went from the room.

* * *

The period that followed the life-altering discovery was a hugely testing time for Hester as she and Connah, by unspoken mutual consent, kept up the fiction that all was well in the Carey Jones household. All three of them went to lunch at Hill Cottage the next day, at Moira's insistence, rather than the formal restaurant lunch Connah had suggested. Fortunately Lowri was so blazingly happy that any constraint between the newly engaged couple went more or less unnoticed during the meal as she gave Moira and Robert a blow-by-blow description of everything she'd done in Tuscany, including a great deal about Andrea.

'But, best of all,' she said with great satisfaction, 'was when I came back from the *Castello* on the last day and Daddy told me he'd asked Hester to marry him. I was so happy I cried like a big baby.' She beamed on the company at large. 'I can't wait to tell Chloe when I get back to school.'

'I hope you don't mind the short notice, Moira,' said Connah, 'but we're aiming for the day before Lowri goes back to school. Hester wants a small party here with you, but please allow me to arrange a caterer.'

Moira's eyes widened as she looked at her daughter. 'You didn't say it would be so soon, Hester.'

'We hadn't sorted the details when I gave you the breaking news.' Hester smiled at Robert. 'Will you mind having people tramping over your garden again?'

'Not in the least, dear.' He patted her hand. 'I'm flattered that you want the reception here. But won't it limit the guest list?'

'My share won't be long,' said Connah.

'My list won't be long either,' Hester assured him. 'The garden is too steep for a marquee, so the numbers will depend on how many can cram into the house if it rains.'

Lowri nodded in a very grown up way. 'But you want the party at home with your Mummy. When I get married I'll want you to do my party too, Hester.'

'Hey—let's sort this wedding first,' said Connah, smiling at her.

The next hurdle was a trip to rural mid-Wales for the formal visit to Bryn Derwen.

Marion Carey Jones came out to meet them as the car moved up a winding drive towards the pillared portico of a solid, four-square house built in the first decade of Victoria's reign. Her silver-streaked hair, cut short to frame her face, had obviously once been as dark as Connah's and, though her finely chiselled features bore traces of her recent ordeal, the likeness to her son was unmistakable. She held out her arms, smiling, as Lowri shot from the car.

'Grandma,' said the child, hugging her, 'we've brought her. This is Hester.'

'How do you do, Mrs Carey Jones?' said Hester, holding out her hand.

The other woman took it, but only to draw Hester nearer so she could kiss her cheek. 'That's such a mouthful, just call me Marion. Welcome, my dear. Connah, take Hester's things up to the guest room. Lowri, run and ask Mrs Powell to bring some tea to the conservatory.'

Having neatly arranged to get Hester to herself for a moment, Marion led the way through to the conservatory at the back of the house.

'No point in beating about the bush—has Connah told you everything now?' she asked without preamble.

Hester nodded. 'In the end he was forced into it, but I'll leave it to him to tell you about that.'

'Has it changed your mind?' asked Marion.

'No. But I wish he'd trusted me with the truth beforehand,' said Hester frankly, then looked round with a smile as Lowri came in with a plate of cakes.

'These are Welsh cakes, Hester. Mrs Powell made them specially.'

'How lovely. They look delicious.'

'Ah, good, Connah,' said his mother as he came in carrying a tea tray. 'You saved Mrs Powell a trip.'

'I don't think she was best pleased,' he said wryly. 'I think she wanted a look at Hester.'

'I'm sure she did. But you can introduce Hester to her later.'

Connah left any mention of Peter Lang until Lowri was in bed that evening after an excellent dinner served early by Mrs Powell who, far from being the ogre Hester had expected, was a trim, neat woman very obviously fond of her employer.

'Her only fault,' said Marion ruefully, once they were sitting in the conservatory later, 'is her fanatical tidiness. She doesn't like trespassers in her kitchen, including Lowri.'

'It's your kitchen, Mother,' Connah reminded her.

'It's a long time since I cooked anything there.' She smiled gently at Hester. 'Lowri is obviously delighted at the prospect of having you for a stepmother, my dear, but do I sense some reservations on your part?'

'Hester has doubts about a decision I've made,' said Connah bluntly. 'Please don't get upset, Mother, but you have to know. Peter Lang turned up at the house yesterday, asking for information about Laura.'

'Good heavens!' Marion's eyes widened, but she took the news calmly, to Hester's relief.

'Unfortunately,' Connah continued grimly, 'he arrived before I had time to tell Hester the truth about Laura.'

'Which, of course,' his mother informed him, 'you should have done before asking her to marry you.'

'I know,' he said bitterly.

'How on earth did Peter Lang find you?'

Connah explained, but she frowned as he mentioned the incident in the park. 'I made Lowri promise not to tell you.'

Marion Carey Jones gave her son a disapproving look. 'Making a child complicit in deceit is not a good thing, Connah.'

'I'm well aware of that. But at the time I was afraid to jeopardise your recovery.'

Her eyes softened. 'So what happened when you finally met Peter Lang yesterday? How did he take the news that he has a daughter?'

Hester tensed and at any other time would have felt amused by the look of guilt on Connah's face.

'I didn't tell him, Mother,' he said brusquely.

Marion Carey Jones looked long and hard at her son. 'So when are you seeing him again?'

'I have no plans to do that.'

She stiffened. 'Are you telling me that you intend to leave him in ignorance?'

'Yes—as Laura wished,' he said flatly.

His mother looked at him searchingly. 'Laura's wishes or yours, Connah?'

'Both. That's my decision, Mother, and it's not open to discussion. Now, if you'll both excuse me, I'm going to check on Lowri.' Connah gave both women a slight formal bow and strode out of the room.

'Are you all right, Marion?' said Hester anxiously.

'Yes. Don't worry. My heart's doing fine, other than feeling heavy right now.' Marion Carey Jones sighed deeply. 'Tell me how you feel about all this, Hester.'

'I don't feel entitled to have a say in it, but personally I think Connah's wrong.'

'I could see that. Does it make you want to back out of the marriage?'

Hester shook her head. 'Has Connah told you how we first met?'

'When your home provided shelter from the storm for my children?' Marion smiled. 'Yes. When he finally brought Laura home to me, Connah was full of gratitude to your mother, though, to be truthful, he didn't mention you at the time.'

Hester smiled ruefully. 'To Connah I was just the teenager who fetched and carried trays. But I fell madly in love with him the moment I set eyes on him, convinced that the lady with him must be his lover and they were running away together. I thought it was wildly romantic.'

'Whereas the truth was anything but.' Marion frowned. 'I want you to know that I strongly disapprove of my son's keeping it from you until after you'd agreed to marry him. Would you have refused if you'd known beforehand?'

'No,' said Hester honestly. 'When I met Connah again I realised why none of the relationships I'd had with men had ever come to anything. Though,' she added hastily, 'I never thought of marrying Connah. Especially after he told me that part of him had died along with Lowri's mother. But when he proposed I accepted, because I love him.'

'A powerful reason for saying yes—my son's a lucky man,' said Marion with warm approval. 'But you disapprove of keeping Peter Lang in the dark.'

'Yes.'

'But not enough to keep you from marrying Connah?'

'Of course not,' said Connah as he rejoined them. 'She won't back out, Mother, because of Lowri. Hester cares a great deal more for my daughter than she does for me.'

'Is that true, Hester?' asked Marion.

'No, it's not.' Hester gave Connah a sidelong look. 'We are both going into this marriage with our priorities firmly in place. As Connah told me right from the start, his requirements are respect and liking—'

'And a third element I shall leave out to save your blushes, Mother,' he said sardonically.

'Talk of sex doesn't make me blush,' she retorted. 'It would all seem rather cold and businesslike otherwise.'

Connah shook his head. 'My future wife is blonde, beautiful, intelligent and loves my daughter. She can even cook. What more can a man ask?'

His mother eyed him thoughtfully. 'And are you what Hester asks for in a husband?'

'I'm not a bad prospect,' said Connah, looking directly at Hester. 'I have my own teeth, reasonable looks and I can support a wife very comfortably. Hester says she likes and respects me—'

'Do you, Hester?' Marion cut in.

'Yes, very much.' Hester looked Connah in the eye. 'But if you have any more secrets I want you to tell me now, not after we're married.'

'Nothing else, I promise. What you see is what you get.' His eyes narrowed. 'So is the wedding still on?'

'Of course,' she said, surprised. 'Why? Are you having second thoughts?'

'Connah is probably afraid that the trouble with Mr Lang has given *you* second thoughts, Hester,' said his mother, and got up. 'I shall take myself to bed. Put the time alone to good use.' She kissed them both and smiled lovingly at Connah as he held the door open for her.

'Let me see you upstairs, Mother,' he urged.

'No need. I do very well if I take my time. You stay with Hester. Goodnight.'

Connah watched her go for a moment, then closed the door and turned to look at Hester. 'What do you suppose my mother meant by putting the time to good use? Rather than fall on each other with ravening lust, I suppose she means we should talk—about Lang, of course. Did she ask you to use persuasion to change my mind?'

Hester held his eyes steadily. 'No, she did not.'

'But that's what she wants. I know my mother only too well.' Connah shrugged. 'I need a Scotch. What would you like? Unless Mrs Powell is a secret drinker, there should be some wine left from dinner.'

'Perfect. Thank you.'

How civilised they were, thought Hester later, as they sat, uneasily silent, with their drinks.

'Look,' said Connah at last, 'you can back out if you want. Lowri would get over it in time.'

Hester put her drink down, startled. 'Is that what *you* want?'

'Of course it's not,' he said explosively, jumping to his feet. 'I'll show you what I want, Hester.' He pulled her up into his arms to kiss her until her head reeled. When he raised his head at last, his eyes blazed into hers. 'I think the ravening lust is a very good idea.'

Hester gave him a smile so radiant that he blinked. 'So do I.'

With a groan of thanksgiving, Connah picked her up and sat down with her in his lap, kissing her with mounting heat that she responded to helplessly, giddy with relief as they drew back from the abyss which had suddenly yawned between them.

He tore his mouth from hers at last and buried his face in her hair. 'This is torture,' he gasped as she clutched him closer. He raised his head to look down into her dazed eyes and smiled in pure male triumph. 'You want me!'

'Yes,' she simply. 'But not here on your mother's sofa.'

'My room's on the top floor, well away from the rest. Share it with me!'

Hester sighed as she slid off his lap to sit beside him. 'I will one day. But not tonight.'

'I didn't think so,' he said with regret, and put his arm round her. 'Now you see why I'm in such a hurry to tie the knot.'

Hester understood his physical needs only too well. Nevertheless, she couldn't help wondering if part of his urgency was the need to form a stable family unit in case Peter Lang found out about Lowri one day and demanded his rights as her biological father. But she kept that thought to herself, reluctant to disrupt the new-found harmony between them. Right now it was enough to be close to Connah in every way, physical and mental. No one, Peter Lang included, could be allowed to spoil the dream that had come true for her when Connah asked her to marry him.

CHAPTER TWELVE

AFTER the return to Albany Square the days passed in a hectic round of shopping for wedding finery and less exciting items like school shoes. To leave himself free for the honeymoon, Connah went down to London to work with John Austin, but immediately after he got back he asked Moira if she would take care of Lowri the next day while he took Hester to buy an engagement ring.

Once Lowri was safely delivered by Sam to spend the day at Hill Cottage, Connah took Hester first to a jeweller and then to lunch at the best restaurant in town.

'Champagne at this time of day?' said Hester.

'To celebrate the occasion. I won't be buying another engagement ring in this life,' he said, filling her glass.

Though the meal was superb, Hester felt too excited to eat much as she gazed down at the cluster of sapphires and diamonds on her finger.

'Not hungry?' asked Connah.

'Not really. Perhaps you'll bring me to this lovely place another time when I'm not so wired.' She smiled at him wryly. 'It's all a bit hard to believe. Not so long ago, my life was other people's babies—'

'Whereas now you're going to marry me and have some of your own,' he said matter-of-factly.

Hester smiled crookedly. 'We hadn't discussed that side of things.'

'No,' he agreed. 'But now the subject's come up, you do realise that Lowri will never stop nagging us until we provide her with a sibling. Or two.'

She nodded, resigned. 'I do, only too well.'

'And your main aim in life is to make Lowri happy!'

'I'd like to make you happy too.'

'In that case, let's go home.'

'But you've hardly touched your champagne,' she protested.

'With reason, so I could drive you home. Right now,' he added, his eyes smouldering into hers.

'You planned this in advance?' Hester asked when they were on their way back to Albany Square.

'No. Once Sam rang me to say that Moira had asked him to stay on to lunch at Hill Cottage it was a case of *carpe diem*. I seized the rare opportunity of the house to ourselves for an hour.'

'So you plied me with champagne,' she accused, laughing.

'Only enough to relax you, my darling.'

The endearment did far more to further his cause than the champagne. Hester's excitement mounted unbearably once they were inside the silent house. Connah took her hand to hurry her up past the study to his bedroom on the next floor, then picked her up and carried her over to the bed.

'I want you so much, Hester,' he said, looking down at her with heat which melted her bones. 'And not just for love in the afternoon, though God knows at this moment I want to throw you on that bed and keep you there until tomorrow.'

'Not tomorrow,' she said with regret. 'Lowri will be back at four.'

Connah gave a shout of laughter and collapsed with her on the bed, and suddenly they were in a tearing, laughing hurry, kissing wildly as they undressed each other with impatient hands. But once they were naked in each other's arms Connah took in a deep, relishing breath of pure satisfaction as his eyes roved over the curves gilded by the sunlight slanting through the blinds. When looking was no longer enough he began to touch, his lips following his inciting hands until, at last, her senses heightened to fever pitch Hester could bear no more.

'Now,' she ordered gruffly, so imperious that Connah obeyed with a smooth, impaling thrust and caught his breath as her inner muscles tightened round him, her smoky blue eyes gleaming almost black with satisfaction. His kiss devoured her as he moved inside her and Hester moved with him, her response so heated that, for the first time in his life, Connah Carey Jones lost control, and all too soon they were gasping in each other's arms, joined in the hot, throbbing rapture of orgasm.

Hester stayed utterly still, happy for a while just to lie there with Connah's body pinning her down, but at last he heaved himself over on his side and she drew in a deep, reviving breath.

'We have another hour,' he informed her, his eyes possessive.

She gave him a sleepy smile. 'Excellent. Because I've lost the will to move.'

'Then we should stay exactly where we are.'

She stretched luxuriously. 'This is a very comfortable bed.'

'Since you'll be sharing it with me in future, I'm glad you like it. I have a comfortable bed in London too,' he added. 'When we stay at the flat on our way back from Italy you can give me your opinion.'

Hester shivered as his lips moved down the curve of her neck to her shoulder. 'I look forward to sleeping on it.'

'Don't bank on too much sleeping. I made my requirements about that side of our marriage very plain, if you remember.'

'I do.' She rolled over to face him. 'How about mine?'

He smoothed a hand down her face. 'Tell me what they are and I'll do my best to fulfil them.'

'I like this part of it a lot,' she said with candour. 'But I want more from our marriage than just sharing a bed or a dinner table, or even providing Lowri with a stepmother, much as I love her. I want to be part of your other life too, Connah. Or don't you think I'm up for that?'

He drew back, frowning. 'What do you mean?'

She smiled crookedly. 'Because I'm blonde and not bad-looking and make my living by caring for children, some men tend to take the package at face value and ignore the brain inside it.'

'Then they're fools,' he said flatly. 'While I was waiting for Laura to recover all those years ago your mother talked a lot about you—how hard you'd worked to help make the guest house a success. Also about your headmistress's disappointment over your choice of career,' he added.

Hester stared at him in surprise. 'She didn't tell me that.' Her mother had never talked much about the mysterious Mr Jones at all. But that, Hester knew, was because Moira had been fully aware that her child was languishing over a man who was not only right out of her league in years and sophistication, but belonged to someone else.

'So, quite apart from my bed, *cariad*, I'm only too happy to have you share every aspect of my life.' His eyes shadowed. 'I won't pretend I've lived like a monk since I took responsibility for Lowri, but I've steered clear of anything remotely like a close relationship. I sublimated myself in work instead. But these past weeks with you in Italy showed me what life could be with a companion like you to share it, and maybe even give me the child of my own I'd never realised I wanted until I met you again.' He pulled her close, a wry look in his eyes. 'Something just struck me.'

'I suppose you mean it's time to get up,' she said, sighing.

'No.' He kissed the hand which wore his ring. 'The moment I put that on your finger, I rushed you home to bed. I swear I wasn't demanding thanks, Hester.'

She grinned. 'Just as well, because I haven't actually said thank you yet.'

'Yes, you have—without words,' he whispered, his breath hot against her skin. 'So thank me again—in exactly the same way!'

The remaining days of Lowri's summer vacation flew by in preparations for the wedding. Connah went back to London for a while to his new restoration project, and this time Lowri made no objection because most of her time was spent at Hill Cottage, helping to get the garden ready for the wedding. She worked so hard that Robert soon presented her with her own fork, trowel and gloves.

'Brilliant! I really enjoy gardening,' she told him, delighted, as she thanked him.

'But you must wear the gloves, darling,' said Moira. 'Otherwise you'll have grimy hands with that lovely blue dress at the wedding.'

'Right then, everybody,' said Hester. 'Since you're all so busy here, I'd like to pop down into town for half an hour for a spot of personal shopping.'

Lowri looked up, frowning. 'But Sam's taken the car back to Albany Square.'

'I'll go in my own, darling. I won't be long.'

'Good, because we'll have lunch out here when you get back,' said Moira. 'If you'd like a break from gardening, Lowri, you can help me make sandwiches.'

Lowri eyed the flower bed she was weeding, obviously torn between her choices. 'I'll finish this bed after lunch then, Robert, if that's all right.'

'Absolutely,' he said affectionately. 'Go inside and have a cold drink, pet. You look hot.'

Hester was glad to be alone for once as she went into town. The particular shopping she had in mind was a secret she had no intention of sharing with anyone. To have something to show for her trip when she got back, Hester treated herself to some shamefully expensive cosmetics, then called in at Albany Square to hide her secret purchases. To her surprise, Connah opened the door when she announced herself.

'You're back!' she exclaimed, delighted, but her smile faded abruptly when he pulled her inside and refused to let her say a word until they were upstairs in the study with the door slammed shut behind them.

'I had a visitor today,' he announced in a tone which made her blood run cold.

No kiss, not even a hello? Hester made herself look at him in polite enquiry. 'Someone I know?'

'She certainly knows you. Her name is Caroline Vernon.' His eyes stabbed hers. 'But her maiden name was Lang. She's Peter Lang's sister.'

Hester frowned. 'And she came *here*? Why?'

His eyes stabbed into hers. 'Because you had a cosy little chat with her about Lowri while you were buying wedding finery.'

Hester stared at him blankly, too surprised at first to be furious. 'I most certainly did not!'

Connah looked sceptical. 'Then how else does the lady know that Lowri is Welsh for Laura, also that you were going to be Lowri's stepmother?'

Were? Past tense?

Hester stared at him angrily. 'Look, Connah, I don't know any Caroline Vernon. Nor do I know how she heard about Lowri. But it certainly wasn't from me. Or from my mother either, in case you're about to accuse her as well.'

'Which just leaves Lowri.' Connah eyed her with distaste. 'Surely you can take the blame for this yourself, Hester, rather than accuse a child?'

'You're doing the accusing, not me,' she said hotly, determined not to cry. 'I don't know this Vernon woman. If she says I told her she's lying. But if you prefer to believe her rather than me, that is, of course, your privilege. And now, if you'll let the prisoner out of the dock, I'm due back at Hill Cottage for lunch.'

'Lunch can wait,' he retorted. 'Perhaps you'd like to know the rest of the conversation.'

'Not really, but you're obviously going to tell me,' said Hester bitterly.

'She told me that her brother was utterly devastated when I told him Laura was dead. So when she rang him to say she'd seen Lowri, he sent her here to plead his cause. Next time he's in this country he craves the privilege of meeting my daughter, who is— I quote—a living reminder of the love of his life,' finished Connah with furious distaste. 'Do you think the man actually had the gall to say that, or was his sister trying to butter me up?'

'So are you going to let him see Lowri, Connah?' asked Hester.

'Like hell I am. For God's sake, Hester, he was married to someone else when he made my sister pregnant!'

Hester held her ground. 'I know that. But he obviously loved Laura very deeply. You said yourself that he kept on trying to see her.'

'But she wouldn't let him near her, remember. Lang not only made her pregnant, he broke Laura's heart. As far as I'm concerned, he as good as killed her.' Connah's eyes hardened. 'I'm not going to let him near her child.'

'Even though she's his child too?'

'No. Because, in every way that matters, she's mine.' Connah seized her by the shoulders. 'You swore you'd never tell Lang about Lowri, but obviously you didn't think that bound you when it came to his sister. What the hell possessed you to confide in the woman, Hester?'

'I did nothing of the kind. I don't *know* his sister.' She freed herself angrily, glaring at him to hide her desperate hurt. 'I didn't talk to anyone other than Lowri, my mother and the shop assistant while I tried on the dress—my wedding gown, incidentally. Perhaps I can get my money back,' she added bitterly and turned her back on him to run down the stairs to the front door, but Connah caught up with her before she reached it and held her by the wrist.

'What the hell do you mean by that?'

'Take an educated guess!'

Connah paled, refusing to let go when she tried to shrug his hand off.

'Lowri will be worried. I've got to go,' she snapped, without looking at him.

'We'll talk later, when she's in bed,' he said grimly.

Which was so much more a threat than a promise, that Hester arrived at Hill Cottage later with very little memory of having driven there.

Hester spent the rest of the afternoon giving the performance of her life, and where Robert and Lowri were concerned she was successful. Not so with her mother.

'What's up?' Moira murmured, keeping her daughter back for a minute when Sam arrived.

'Bridal nerves,' lied Hester.

'Anything to do with Connah's unexpected return today?'

'It was a surprise, certainly.'

'Not what I asked!' Moira gave her a hug. 'All right. I won't nag. But please ring me tomorrow.'

Because Sam sent a text to say they were on the way as they set off, Connah was waiting for them in the garage when they arrived. Lowri rushed to hug him, chattering like a magpie as they went upstairs.

'I didn't know you were coming back today. I've been helping Robert do the garden, Daddy, and it's going to look so beautiful for the wedding.' She beamed up at him. 'Only a week to go now. Are you excited?'

He smiled at her indulgently. 'Of course I am, even more than you.'

'Not possible,' she said, laughing, and turned to Hester. 'Are you excited too?'

'You bet. Now, off to the bath, Miss Jones. You need a good scrub, and don't forget your hands and nails.' Hester smiled coolly at Connah. 'I didn't expect you, so there's only salad and so on for supper.'

'Fine by me.' He took Lowri by the hand. 'Run up and have your bath, then come back down to me in the study. We'll play chess while Hester gets supper ready.'

Feeling she'd had a stay of execution, Hester prepared the meal as much as she could beforehand, then went up to have a shower. She took her time over her hair, which had gained a few highlights courtesy of the Italian sun, and, feeling in need of war paint for the encounter later, she made-up her face and eyes with more drama than usual.

Conversation over the meal was no problem, since Lowri talked non-stop about the wedding throughout. Connah exchanged a wary glance with Hester now and then and looked, to her intense pleasure, increasingly baffled by the pleasant smiles she gave him in return.

'Chloe rang me today as soon as she got home,' Lowri announced. 'She's been in Cornwall all summer. They've got a house down there. I told her all about the wedding and my bridesmaid dress. She was going to ring Olivia and Daisy right away to tell them, and told me to take loads of wedding pictures back to school with me.'

'I'll inform the photographer of your requirements,' said Connah, lips twitching.

Lowri giggled happily, but Hester eyed him in surprise.

'You've organised a photographer?'

'Of course.' His eyes held hers. 'No wedding is complete without a record of the happy day.'

She gave him one of her brightest smiles. 'I thought you avoided that kind of thing.'

'Ah, but the reason for my reticence no longer applies,' he informed her suavely, and turned to his daughter. 'We'll go back to our chess for half an hour before you go to bed, then you need an early night,' said Connah, and looked at Hester. 'Then later you and I can have some time to ourselves.'

'I expect you want to kiss Hester a lot after being away lately,' said Lowri, nodding sagely. 'Chloe says her dad still kisses her mother all the time. And they've been married for *ages*.' She rushed over to Hester suddenly and threw her arms round her. 'I'm so glad you're going to marry Daddy. I keep pinching myself to make sure I'm not dreaming.'

Later, when Lowri was settled for the night, Hester went back down to the kitchen to make coffee, then took the tray up to the study. Connah got up to stand in front of the empty fireplace, his tanned face tense as he watched her fill the cups. She handed one to him, then sat down with her own and waited in obdurate silence.

When he finally spoke, he said the last thing she expected.

'Hester, I owe you an apology. I asked Lowri tonight if she'd talked to a pretty dark lady when you were choosing dresses, and apparently she did, during a visit to the ladies' room. The woman asked her name, then commented on the lovely blue dress she'd seen Lowri trying on, so of course the child told her all about the wedding. Then Moira arrived to check on Lowri, and the lady vanished.'

'I see,' said Hester evenly. 'Mystery solved.'

Connah put his cup down untouched and sat beside her. 'I'm sorry—desperately sorry—for doubting you, Hester. I expected you to say the wedding was off when you got back tonight.'

'I fully intended to at one point,' she agreed, and felt an ignoble gush of satisfaction when his jaw clenched. 'But it lasted only as far as Hill Cottage, by which time I'd remembered that Lowri would be utterly heartbroken if I changed my mind.'

He winced. 'You mean you'll go through with the wedding just to keep my daughter happy?'

She shrugged. 'There are other reasons.'

He eyed her with uncharacteristic humility. 'Respect and liking?'

'Both of those were in short supply when you accused me of breaking my word,' she informed him tartly, then finished her coffee and stood up to put their cups on the tray.

'Where are you going?' he demanded.

'To bed. It's been a tiring day.'

'Stay for a while—please,' he said, a note of entreaty in his voice which almost soothed her bruised heart. But not quite enough.

She shook her head. 'I need an early night. There's a lot to do between now and Tuesday.'

He strode across the room and took her in his arms. 'At least kiss me goodnight to show you've forgiven me.'

Hester held up her face obediently and Connah crushed her close, kissing her with a passion which left her dizzy and breathless when he raised his head at last.

'Have you?' he said roughly.

'Have I what?'

'Forgiven me.'

She smiled crookedly. 'Not yet. But I'll work on it during my stay at Hill Cottage. I'm going home in the morning, until the wedding. Mother was all for Lowri doing the same, but I thought you'd prefer Sam to bring her over each day to me and fetch her back every evening so you can put her to bed. All this is subject to your approval, of course.'

Connah's eyes burned into hers. 'Retaliation, Hester?'

'Certainly not. I always intended to spend the last few days of single life with my mother.' She shrugged. 'I would have told you that this afternoon as soon as I saw you, but your accusation rather got in the way.'

'I've apologised for that,' he said harshly.

'And I've accepted. Goodnight, Connah.'

Hester sat watching the Chiantigiana unfold before her through Tuscan hills gilded by the setting sun. The views were as breathtaking as before, but this time there was no sleepy little head on her shoulder. She cast a glance at her husband, who drove as he did most things—with skill and concentration. The past few days had passed so quickly in some ways that it was hard to believe that here they were at last, Mr and Mrs Connah Carey Jones, bride and groom, but not husband and wife as yet in the true sense of the word, since the bride had spent part of her wedding night in the bathroom of the master suite, parting with her wedding breakfast.

Connah had been a tower of strength. Ignoring her impassioned pleas to go away and leave her alone, he'd held Hester's head, mopped her clammy face and fed her sips of mineral water until her stomach had finally decided to behave.

'It must have been the prawn canapés,' she said wanly as he tucked her into bed. 'I hope no one else is affected.'

'I'm not concerned with anyone else right now. My mother will see to Lowri if necessary,' Connah said firmly. 'And if you feel no better in the morning she can come with me when I deliver Lowri to the school.'

'No!' Hester struggled upright. 'I'll be better by then. I can have a break at Bryn Derwen when we drop Marion off on the way, but I shall go on to the school with you, no matter how I feel,' she assured him. 'Lowri's got her heart set on showing off her new stepmother. I can sleep on the drive to Heathrow afterwards.'

And it had been worth the effort, thought Hester as Connah negotiated the winding road with due care for his passenger's digestive system. Lowri's delight had been a joy to see as she'd introduced Hester to her friends.

'Almost there,' said Connah, as the familiar village came into sight. 'How do you feel?'

'Tired, but the meal we had at that sweet little trattoria seems to be staying put, thank goodness. ' Hester cast a rueful glance at his profile. 'You were so good last night, Connah. I never even managed to say thank you at the time.'

'What else are husbands for?' he said, smiling crookedly, and turned up the road which led to Casa Girasole.

Flavia had not been required to wait to let them in because Jay Anderson had handed over the key at the wedding. Connah got out of the car to unlock the door, then helped Hester out, eyeing her closely.

'Pale, but very interesting,' he commented, and surprised her by picking her up. 'Standard procedure for brides,' he said casually as he carried her into the house. He set her down with great care, then went back out to bring in the luggage. Hester looked around with a sigh of pleasure. Flavia might not have waited for them but her presence was evident in the vases of flowers everywhere, also in the note on the kitchen table.

'I assume this is about the food she's left for us,' said Hester as Connah joined her. 'My Italian isn't up to it.'

'I don't think mine is either, but you're right about the general message,' he agreed, studying it. 'I'll take the bags upstairs. But I suggest we leave unpacking until the morning. You still look fragile.'

'Not too fragile to carry my overnight bag,' said Hester. 'I'll just check to see what's on offer for breakfast in the morning, though it probably won't be a full English.'

'I'll settle for anything you care to give me,' he told her, meeting her eyes, and went out.

Which was clear enough, thought Hester as she inspected the contents of the refrigerator. Suddenly desperate for a shower, she went upstairs to the room she'd slept in last time and found all their luggage stacked neatly at the foot of the bed. This time her bridegroom was making it clear that he meant to share it with her. She smiled a little. She always knew where she stood with Connah.

He strolled out of the bathroom, looking as good to her as always in a thin shirt and linen trousers only slightly rumpled from the journey. He smiled as he put his wallet and keys down on the dressing table. 'I've left a message for Lowri at the school to let her know we got here. I've put my bath stuff in there, by the way, but you take first turn in the shower while I take a stroll in the garden.'

'Thank you.' She smiled, feeling absurdly shy. 'I'll make some coffee later while you take your turn.'

Connah could have showered in either of the other two bathrooms, but his intention was obviously to share everything from the start. She smiled ruefully. After the enforced intimacies of their unromantic wedding night, there was little left to be shy about.

Hester rang home to tell her mother they'd arrived and afterwards took everything needed for a shower from her overnight bag and got to work. In no mood to spend time styling wet hair, she pulled on a shower cap and stood under the spray only long enough to perk her up a bit. She dried herself rapidly, slapped new, expensive moisturiser all over her body and tugged an almond-pink shift over some of her trousseau underwear. She brushed out her hair, did the bare minimum to her face, then thrust her feet into flat silver sandals and went downstairs in search of her husband, the very word giving her such a buzz that she paused to savour it before going out on to the loggia.

Connah turned with a smile. 'You were quick.'

'I thought you might be as desperate for a shower as I was, so I put a move on.'

He put a finger under her chin. 'You look much better, Hester.'

'I feel much better.' Even with his touch sending shivers down her spine.

'Are you cold?' he demanded.

'Of course not. It's a beautiful evening. Shall we have coffee out here?'

'I've got a better idea. I put a bottle of very expensive champagne on ice—one of a dozen sent over by *Il Conte* as a wedding gift. I found them when I was looking through Jay's wine selection.'

She smiled, surprised. 'How very sweet of Luigi. Is he here at the *Castello*?'

'If he is, I trust he'll have too much tact to come visiting.' Connah raised her hand to his lips and kissed it. 'It is our honeymoon, remember.'

As if she were likely to forget! Hester sighed as she breathed in the night-time scents of the garden when she was alone. The honeymoon had got off to a spectacularly bad start, but from now on she would do her best to see it improved, if only by not throwing up any more.

A moon was silvering the water in the pool when Connah joined her to pour champagne. His hair was wet and slicked back from his face, which looked dark against his white shirt in the light from the shaded lamp on the table.

'A toast, Mrs Carey Jones,' he said, handing her a glass.

She raised it in toast. 'To us.'

'I'll drink to that! To us.' He drank deeply, then moved his chair closer to hers, the lamplight glinting on his wedding ring as he took her hand. 'My ring was a surprise, Hester. I was deeply touched.'

'I wasn't sure you'd care for one, but I bought it anyway.' She smiled a little. 'It was my reason for shopping on my own that afternoon without Lowri. I sneaked back to Albany Square to hide the ring. The last thing I expected was to find you there.'

'Or the accusations I hurled at you.' He raked his hand through his damp hair. 'After the things I said I'm amazed you turned up at the church, though I hoped—prayed—you would, if only for Lowri's sake.'

'Of course I turned up,' she said matter-of-factly. 'When I make a promise I keep it.'

'Twisting the knife?' Connah's fingers linked with hers. 'God knows you have the right. I was a swine to you that day, Hester. But I thought you'd deliberately gone against my wishes on something of such huge importance to me. As well as angry, I was desperately hurt—'

'So was I,' she said with feeling. 'I felt as though my heart was breaking on the drive back to Hill Cottage.'

Connah's grasp tightened painfully. 'Is it back in one piece now?' he said huskily.

'Not yet. You still have some repairing to do!' She smiled at him so cheerfully that he laughed and suddenly they were completely at ease together as they talked over the wedding.

'You were a very beautiful bride,' said Connah.

'I was all for wearing blue like Lowri, but Mother was so adamant you'd want me in something more traditionally bridal I went for ivory chiffon in the end.'

'Moira was absolutely right. Incidentally, it was very good of her—and Robert—to organise everything in their own home, rather than a hotel. The garden at Hill Cottage made the perfect setting for the party afterwards. Lowri was so happy,' said Connah fondly. 'So was I,' he added, 'at least I was once I saw you and Robert walk down the aisle, Hester. Jay couldn't understand why I was so stressed, but right up to the last moment I wasn't sure you'd be there.'

'Well, I was, and here we are,' said Hester and yawned suddenly. 'Sorry!'

Connah got up and drew her to her feet. 'You're tired. Let's lock up and go to bed.'

But at the foot of the stairs he paused to look down at Hester in question. 'Do you want me to take a turn round the garden and give you half an hour to yourself first?'

She grinned. 'Of course not. After last night, Connah, how could I possibly be shy about sharing a room with you?'

'God, I was worried,' he said with feeling as they reached the cool, airy bedroom. 'I was all for calling a doctor.'

'Which caused the first quarrel of our marriage,' she said, rolling her eyes. 'What a night you had.'

'I'm hoping,' he said, straight-faced, 'that tonight will be an improvement.'

'Me too,' she said candidly and gave him a smile of such shameless invitation that Connah scooped her up into his arms and held her so tightly she felt his heart hammering against her.

'Thank God for that,' he said hoarsely, 'though be warned; I want you so much I don't think I can be gentle.'

She shook her head impatiently. 'I don't want gentle. Just love me, Connah.'

'I do. I will!' He sat down with her on his lap, his mouth hot and possessive on hers for a long, breathless interval. At last he stood her on her feet to let her dress fall to the floor, then, without so much as a glance at the underwear she'd chosen so carefully for just this moment, he relieved her of it, then rid himself of his own clothes without letting her go.

'That was clever,' gasped Hester as their naked bodies fell in a tangle together on the bed.

'Desperate, not clever,' he said against her mouth, and kissed her with uncontrolled hunger that thrilled her so much more than any polished, practised caresses could have done that she responded to every touch and caress with a joyous abandon which soon robbed Connah of any last remnants of restraint. He gasped her name against her parted mouth and surrendered to her clamouring hands, thrusting home into hot, tight warmth as their bodies united in a wild careering race to a glorious place they reached almost in unison, straining each other so close they stayed locked together long after the tide of passion had receded to leave them quiet in each other's arms.

Connah raised his dishevelled head at last and looked deep into her dazed eyes. 'Tell me the truth, Hester.'

'I'll try,' she said warily.

He turned on his side, taking her with him so they lay face to face. 'Did you turn up at the church purely for Lowri's sake?'

Relieved, she smoothed the hair back from his forehead and gave him a sleepy smile. 'Of course not. I love Lowri dearly, but I'm not as noble as that. If you want the truth, Connah, wild horses wouldn't have kept me away for the simple reason that I fell madly in love with you the very first time I ever saw you.'

He tensed, staring at her incredulously. 'At the first interview?'

She shook her head. 'Long before that. On a January night ten years ago you smiled at me when I handed over your supper tray, and that was that.'

'But my darling, you were just a child!'

'I was seventeen, Connah, with a full set of female hormones, and you were the archetypal answer to a maiden's prayer.' Hester smiled lovingly. 'The fact that you were unattainable only made it all the more romantic. You were the dream lover who haunted my dreams for years. Then fate took a hand and I answered your advertisement. When you walked into your study that day in Albany Square, I found nothing had changed. I still felt the same about you. So did my hormones, the minute you shook my hand,' she added, eyes glinting. 'So that, Mr Carey Jones, was my reason for marrying you—nothing to do with liking and respect and so on.'

'Thank God for that,' said Connah gruffly, then pulled her close and kissed her, his hand possessive on the curve of her bare hip. 'Tell me again that you love me.'

'You first!'

'Of course I love you,' he growled. 'Why else do you think

the days before the wedding were such hell for me? I was sure, right up to the last minute, that you'd back out.'

'I love you too much to do that.' She kissed him and wriggled closer. 'So was tonight that improvement you wanted?'

'There's room for a lot more improvement yet,' he said, rolling over to capture her beneath him. 'It's a long time until morning.'

On the last night of the honeymoon, when the packing was done and everything was ready for departure in the morning, Hester lay close to her husband, unable to sleep.

'What's wrong?' he said into the quiet darkness.

'I've got a confession to make,' she said reluctantly. 'I should have made it as soon as we arrived, but I was afraid it would spoil our honeymoon.'

Connah reached over to switch on the light, then sat up and drew her up to sit propped beside him. He leaned over to kiss her swiftly, then gave her the bone-melting smile rarely bestowed on anyone other than his wife and child. 'Confess, then,' he said tenderly and brushed a gleaming gold lock of hair back from her forehead. 'Whatever you've done, I forgive you.'

Hester tried to think of some way to lead up to it, but in the end she blurted, 'It wasn't the prawns. I'm pregnant.'

Connah's eyes widened, a look of such delight dawning in them that Hester's filled with tears of pure relief. 'We're having a baby?' he asked incredulously.

She nodded and sniffed inelegantly. 'When I went shopping for your ring that day I also bought a pregnancy testing kit. I'd had my suspicions ever since the holiday here, so I went to the cloakroom in a coffee shop and found I was right.'

'Oh, my darling!' Connah hugged her to him, rubbing his cheek over her hair. 'And you couldn't tell me because I gave you hell the moment I saw you.'

She nodded and burrowed her face into his bare shoulder.

'I meant to tell you before the wedding, but then it occurred to me that you'd think it was my only reason for turning up. So I decided to leave it until I'd proved to you exactly why I married you.'

He turned her face up to his. 'Because you love me!'

'Always,' she said shakily, then gave him a crooked little smile. 'And it occurred to me that if you knew you might be wary of making love to me very much.'

'God, yes,' he said with feeling, thinking of the passionate hours they'd spent together in this very bed. He slid down to press his lips against her flat stomach. 'I hope all's well in there.'

'Of course it is!' Hester yawned suddenly. 'Sorry. Will you cuddle me to sleep?'

Connah moved back up the bed to hold her close. 'Tonight and every night,' he assured her, then chuckled. 'Let's make the most of it while we can.' He kissed her tenderly. 'Goodnight, wife.'

'Goodnight, husband.' Hester settled down happily to sleep, but after a while Connah whispered her name.

'What's the matter?' she asked sleepily.

'You were right.'

'I'm always right,' she assured him, 'but what about in this particular instance?'

'Now I'm going to have a child of my own, I feel a pang of sympathy for Lang. Not a huge one, admittedly, but enough to contact him when we get back, and tell him he can meet Lowri next time he's in the country.'

Hester clutched his hand tightly, her eyes filling with tears. 'Darling! What a lovely idea.'

'I thought you'd be pleased. But I'll say he's an old friend of her mother's,' he said, thinking it over. 'Then maybe, some time in the future, when she's seen him from time to time and she's old enough to cope, she can be told the truth—Darling, don't cry!'

'Sorry,' said Hester thickly. 'Expectant mothers tend to get emotional.'

'Expectant fathers too,' he said huskily, and kissed her tears away as he held her close. 'I know the perfect way to cheer you up,' he added after a time.

Hester wriggled closer, sniffing inelegantly. 'What is it?'

'Just picture Lowri's face when we tell her about the baby!'

The big miniseries from

HARLEQUIN Presents

Dare you read it?

Bedded by Blackmail
Forced to bed...then to wed?

He's got her firmly in his sights and she's got
only one chance of survival—surrender to his
blackmail...and him...in his bed!

THE ITALIAN
RAGS-TO-RICHES WIFE
by *Julia James*
Book # 2716

Laura Stowe has something Allesandro di Vincenzo wants,
and he must grit his teeth and charm her into his bed, where
she will learn the meaning of desire....

Available April 2008 wherever books are sold.

Don't miss more titles in the
BEDDED BY BLACKMAIL series—coming soon!

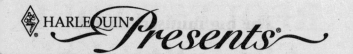

REQUEST YOUR FREE BOOKS!

HARLEQUIN *Presents* ®

2 FREE NOVELS PLUS 2 FREE GIFTS!

PASSION GUARANTEED SEDUCTION

HP07

I ♥ HARLEQUIN® *Presents*

BROUGHT TO YOU BY FANS OF HARLEQUIN PRESENTS.

We are its editors and authors and biggest fans—and we'd love to hear from YOU!

Subscribe today to our online blog at www.iheartpresents.com

HARLEQUIN *Presents*

Private jets. Luxury cars. Exclusive five-star hotels.
Designer outfits for every occasion and an entourage
to see to your every whim...

In this brand-new collection,
ordinary women step into the
world of the super-rich and are

TAKEN BY
THE MILLIONAIRE

Don't miss the glamorous collection:

MISTRESS TO THE TYCOON
by **NICOLA MARSH**

AT THE BILLIONAIRE'S BIDDING
by **TRISH WYLIE**

THE MILLIONAIRE'S
BLACKMAIL BARGAIN
by **HEIDI RICE**

HIRED FOR THE BOSS'S BED
by **ROBYN GRADY**

Available March 11
wherever books are sold.

HARLEQUIN *Presents*

He's successful, powerful—and extremely sexy....
He also happens to be her boss! Used to getting his
own way, he'll demand what he wants from her—
in the boardroom and the bedroom....

Watch the sparks fly as these couples
work together—and play together!

IN BED WITH
THE BOSS

Don't miss any of the stories in April's collection!

MISTRESS IN PRIVATE
by **JULIE COHEN**

IN BED WITH HER ITALIAN BOSS
by **KATE HARDY**

MY TALL DARK GREEK BOSS
by **ANNA CLEARY**

HOUSEKEEPER TO
THE MILLIONAIRE
by **LUCY MONROE**

Available April 8
wherever books are sold.

www.eHarlequin.com